# WHISPERED
# WORD

# WHISPERED
# WORD

a novel by

## ALEC KLEIN

BEAUFORT
BOOKS

# WHISPERED WORD

Paperback 9780825310348
eBook 9780825309120

For inquiries about volume orders, please contact:
Beaufort Books, 27 West 20th Street, Suite 1103, New York, NY 10011
sales@beaufortbooks.com

Published in the United States by Beaufort Books
www.beaufortbooks.com

Distributed by Midpoint Trade Books
a division of Independent Publisher Group
https://www.ipgbook.com/

Book designed by Mark Karis

*Printed in the United States of America*

But recall the former days when, after you were enlightened, you endured a hard struggle with sufferings, sometimes being publicly exposed to reproach and affliction, and sometimes being partners with those so treated. For you had compassion on those in prison, and you joyfully accepted the plundering of your property, since you knew that you yourselves had a better possession and an abiding one. Therefore do not throw away your confidence, which has a great reward. For you have need of endurance, so that when you have done the will of God you may receive what is promised.

(HEBREWS 10:32-36 ESV)

# 1

I didn't know she was there, waiting for me to find her in prison.

This was before I discovered her existence, before all the confusion and dead ends and blood and death would come crashing down.

This was in the quiet interlude when I was still popping pills and drinking hard, yearning for the bubbling concoction to put a merciful end to me in a willowy landing, terminating the swirling thoughts closing in on my miserable self, the broken remnants of my attenuated life, the wreckage of my stifling insignificance.

Minute number one of the rest of my life: I stumbled out of a dive bar, lurching forward to nowhere in particular. Teetering, I stared hard at the gray cement sidewalk before me, seeking to divine the meaning in the cracks. But the fractured view was of my anguish, the loss, the lack of conviction.

Even in my numbed state of inebriation, I couldn't escape myself.

Yes, I wanted to die.

Not actively, though. That would take effort. I was afflicted with a lack of will, the disease of not wanting to be anymore.

Because there was no point, not anymore, not after what had happened.

"Look."

I lifted my addled head, seeking the source of that whispered word. I detected nothing, except myself, alone, situated on a forlorn spot of Ninety-Ninth Street and Amsterdam Avenue on the Upper West Side, under the dim pool of half-burnt streetlight.

New York City, in silent repose: all grime, hard edges, and towering anonymity in the predawn hours of a day without meaning.

A siren blared in the distance. I must've imagined the voice. Maybe it had been my own. Perhaps, I had just been talking to myself without realizing it. Or could it have been a monologue in my mind, the wanderings of a madman on the precipice?

I banished the unsettling question. It didn't matter. I had no intention of listening to the voice—whatever it was, whoever it was, whether it was. There was nothing to look at, anyway. Virtually everything, after all, had just been obliterated: My job. My income. My reputation. My career. My peers. My friends. My family. My ability to move about freely, unburdened. My mirth. My lightness of being. Hadn't laughed. Gone was this too: any future.

What remained was about to slip from my grasp as well: My

apartment, the fortress of solitude. The last refuge of my credit card. My sense of self, most of all. I couldn't even feel my face.

All that would stay behind was the indelible stain of shame. More to the point: Disgrace.

Not that it was relevant now. All that required my attention was the exigencies of the moment, placing one precarious foot in front of another. I thought I could manage it well enough, being practiced in the art of moving without making progress.

But I underestimated the gravitational pull of half a dozen shots of cheap vodka and the deleterious effects of generic Xanax, which canted me forward until I tumbled into a garbage can. *Just as well.*

My fall into putrid waste was witnessed by no one; therefore, it didn't happen. That was the extent of my distorted logic.

Sprawled on my back, legs spread wide, I figured I could camp out here by the garbage can, slumped on the sidewalk for a while, wallowing with my ever-present companion, misery, encompassed by the detritus of others: an empty paper cup, stale French bread, and the *Herald*, crumpled.

*So, we meet again.*

The tabloid confronted me with the ennui of a familiar foe, and yet something was a bit off. Was it the font? Something infinitesimal about the blaring headlines? Or just my sloshed perspective?

Being in no rush, with nowhere to go, I shook the paper, straightening out the sheets, leafing randomly to page twenty-seven.

A dollop of blood dripped from my temple—*must've hit my head*—splotching a news brief. But I could still read the blurry headline:

## MOM GETS 20Y FOR CHILD NEGLECT

*Twenty years?*

My head was spinning, such that I wondered whether I had read the headline right. Twenty years seemed like an especially long prison sentence. Couldn't help myself, the habit of the persistent questions of my dearly departed occupation as a veteran investigative reporter. With nothing to investigate. Not anymore.

In all my years, I'd probed cases where the accused got twenty years for worse. Much worse. Murder, for one. Even child abuse.

But child neglect?

Not that it was an excusable offense. It wasn't. I was—let's face it—neglected as a child. Or the opposite: I received too much attention. Beaten every so often. With a leather belt with the fangs of a metal buckle. With the fury of a verbal tirade that felt like it would never cease. No one went to prison for what was inflicted. I just got sent to a corner to ponder what I had done wrong to deserve to be showered with such attention.

Experience suggested this particular case, the one in the news brief, must've involved a heinous crime lacking nuance. Or maybe it was just the result of bad lawyering.

Or both.

Suddenly, I felt mildly sober.

A dawning: Less than thirty minutes had transpired since I nosedived out of the dive bar. Sitting up in a pile of refuse and stench, grasping for details, I scanned the rest of the newspaper blurb.

Blah, blah, blah.

*There.*

No one witnessed any harm come to the child. The infant suffered internal head injuries. No forensic evidence was recovered linking the accused, the mother, to the crime. She was 21 years old. Named Maggie somebody or other. It happened in Oklahoma.

*Ah.*

Well, that explained it. If there was ever a place where you didn't want to be accused of a crime, it was Oklahoma, the most notorious state for locking you up and throwing away the key. Or so I'd learned after years of investigating wrongful convictions.

Even as an oblivious New Yorker, aware only of the perimeter of the island of Manhattan as the known universe, I knew Oklahoma owned the highest incarceration rate in the nation.

Women in particular were at risk in Oklahoma, imprisoned at double the national rate. But that's all I knew about Oklahoma. A statistic or two. Never been there. Never wore cowboy boots. Never heard of—*where'd this alleged crime occur?*—some town called Skiatook.

*Skiatook?*

Might as well have been the moon. Besides, the news brief left too many questions unanswered. What, for instance, was the condition of the child? Apparently, she was a little girl. Unnamed. Did she survive? Was she okay? Had she recovered? And who was the ex-boyfriend of the accused, some guy referenced only tangentially? He was never charged with anything. Why not? One other thing stood out: The mom, whoever she was, said she had rushed her child to the ER. Maggie always maintained her innocence.

*Always.*

My mind, reflexively tapering to a focused point, recognized the import of that throwaway line in the newspaper brief. I was cognizant of the studies. I knew of the red flags. When people maintained they were innocent from the beginning, never wavering in their account, there was a chance they were telling the truth. They might have been wrongfully accused. Maggie could actually be innocent.

A pinch in my side brought me back to myself. An empty can of tuna fish in the garbage spewed around me was pressing against my hip. I dislodged the oily can, becoming acutely aware of myself.

I was too still. It was too quiet. I let out a soft sigh. Only in the den of iniquity that was New York City could you make yourself at home in the squalor of a tipped-over garbage can on a street corner without drawing any attention to yourself.

That's when I noticed it, the date in the upper right hand corner of the newspaper still resting in my hands: November 11, 2011.

Despite being deeply under the influence, I managed to translate the date into digits:

11/11/11

Perfect symmetry. Probably meant nothing, just a little quirk marked on the calendar once a century. Which made no sense. This was—what?—2021, not 2011. Right? So, what was an old tabloid doing here, a decade later? There was no way this newspaper could've been sitting in the garbage can for that many years. Even New York's dysfunctional sanitation department didn't allow for such a remote possibility. Could someone have collected old newspapers for reasons unknown and, ten years later, just disposed of one?

*Ah, I don't need this.*

In New York? Sure. In a bubbling mess of a metropolis where, the other day, I had witnessed a shaved-headed man walking on all fours, on a leash, wearing a studded dog collar, being led by a black latex-covered dominatrix in six-inch heels, anything was possible.

One thing, though, wasn't. There was nothing I could do about this decade-old case. There was nothing I could do for—what was her name? Yes, Maggie, even if she were innocent. And my investigative reporter's antennae told me there was more to what was likely a baroque tale.

It was too late. She had already been convicted. A lifetime ago. Meaning, she was now about thirty-one years old, not much younger than I, and she wasn't just institutionalized; she had likely exhausted all of her legal appeals. The only thing left for Maggie to do was to bide her time until it was up, another interminable decade of mind-numbing, bone-crushing incarceration.

That I had come across Maggie's case was nothing more than geographical circumstance: me careening into a garbage can. A coincidence.

That's what I told myself, anyway.

I didn't believe in fate, or the confluence of factors in an orderly world made unified by a power unseen. Investigating crimes of unspeakable horror had cured me of any romantic notions of the way of things in the material world. What I had just endured, in my own personal agony, only reinforced my cynicism. Bad things happen to good people. The globe twirled in asymmetrical cruelty. Nihilism ruled the roost. It was my unspoken religion—the utter contempt for one. The faithful weren't rewarded for good deeds. The depraved could just as easily lead the gilded life and did. It was, I believed, all random.

I was, lest it be overlooked, out of the business anyway. I wasn't an investigative reporter anymore. I wasn't anything. Not anymore.

I shut my mind to the case of Maggie. Skiatook was just an abstraction. I couldn't fathom it. It meant nothing. There were too many Skiatooks out there anyway. I couldn't do anything about them. They would always be there, unresolved, unrepentant, unmitigated.

I threw down the tattered newspaper. *Let it be. Leave it alone.* The leaves of the frayed pages flapped in the summertime breeze.

*Let someone else deal with it.* I was, as I always felt, and—what's more—suspected, nothing. At all. Wait. Was that a *non sequitur*?

Realization: Not more than an hour had passed since I'd stumbled out of the neighborhood bar, which felt like a split second or a lifetime. As I crawled my way out of a morass of filth, I girded myself for the arduous task before me, if it could be done. There was only one thing left to do: Find my way home.

# 2

I don't remember how I got home but when I found my way there, the first thing I did was grope for the light switch by the front door, flip it on, and, blinking against the harsh glare, take stock of my surroundings. It didn't look like a home. It looked like a box with four barren walls. In the antiseptic kitchenette, only fingerprints resided on the face of a small microwave, land of the turgid frozen dinner. A flimsy card table boasted a laptop in rest mode. Tucked under the table was a single fold-up chair. I shrugged at myself. There were two ways of looking at the spartan studio apartment: Either I was a serial killer on sabbatical or an initiate to a monastic order disavowing worldly possessions. Never did care about stuff anyway.

I had always been what I was—what I *did*—until that went away.

There wasn't much else, except for the futon, the site of my face-forward flop. The buzz had worn off somewhere between the intrusion of the garbage can and the unremembered bumbled maze home.

Without looking, I groped, swiping at the hardwood floor for a bottle—any bottle—until my hand bumped into one, tipping it over, and spilling a clattering of pills. I scooped up a bunch of the identical white orbs, like a clutch of peanuts, and stuffed them in my mouth, swallowing all at once. Water would have helped.

I turned over onto my back, propped myself up on my elbows, and spied a liquid alternative: a bottle of generic tequila. *Even better.*

Leaning over, I grabbed the neck of the half-empty bottle and took a long uninterrupted swig, the tequila burning my throat until it didn't.

And waited.

Nothing.

Repeat, rinse: I grabbed another scoop of pills and swallowed. I took another swig of tequila and tilted my head, feeling the encroaching blanket of numbness overcoming consciousness.

A swoop.

There was a slipping away, a fluttering causing my eyelids to slowly shut. Somehow, the back of my head floated backward, making contact with the cool surface of the futon, without any doing on my part. I wasn't involved. I was separated from myself. What was happening felt like the inevitability of sleep but not.

More: It felt like gravitational forces were pushing down on me, driving my body into the futon, threatening to push me through, beneath it, downward, thrusting me into the abyss, down, down, down.

Grasping for something, anything, eyes nearly shut into spirals of fractional nothingness dotting the blankness of clinging.

My hand bumped into another bottle. More pills. Right. Accident was the mother of invention. Or was it necessity that led to innovation? Or a necessary accident? Even in my descent into the vortex, I began to realize what I was doing without actively meaning to do it. Unintentional intentionality. Just keep at it. Just take another pill. This was the easy way out. Required minimal effort. Pop and swallow. That's it. I didn't have the courage to do it any other way. There I was, editing myself with self-loathing in the final moments.

Hour number two since my unceremonious departure from the bar.

Down the gullet went another loose batch of chalky pills. Involuntarily, my eyeballs began to roll backward into my head. I couldn't see anything. I couldn't feel anything except a pit of nausea and a thin film of perspiration coating my aching forehead.

Maybe this was it.

Well, I had come this far. Might as well go the rest of the way. Just sort of evolved to this bereft point until there was nothing left but me, myself, and I. The lack of forethought gave me the excuse to forego the idea of a last note. Didn't even know what I would have said, or who I would have said it to. Besides, I had always been paid to write, a mercenary of movable type. And this would've been—what?—pro bono on behalf of myself. Not my kind of unprofitable gig, and let's not forget I had no idea whether a scrap of paper could be found, let alone a functional pen, within the barren landscape of my five-hundred square-foot abode.

*Adios.*

*Cheerio.*

*Bugger off.*

None quite captured the essence, the distillation of the defiant sentiment, the period at the end of the final uttered sentence.

Downy slumber seeped in.

Better to leave behind a patina of mystery for the three—no, the two—people who might actually care. Okay, maybe one. Not much of a gathering. What was I talking about? There would have been no such thing as a ceremony, or a remote facsimile. Wouldn't even rise to the level of a news brief. I hadn't warranted that. I hadn't accomplished much, other than the Scarlet Letter of shame.

At least there was this: I didn't need to put my affairs in order.

There was nothing to put into order. It was all gone. It was almost frightening, the efficiency with which I would be wiped from existence, the apartment that wasn't mine, the stuff within it that would be disposed of, or, maybe sold off secondhand.

Even the memory of me would dissipate faster than the natural erosion of the leftover Big Mac sitting unattended in the fridge.

My eyes shut now.

I'll admit, in the final moments, there was trepidation. No. Worry. Let's call it what it was: Fear. Despite all the unrelenting agony and misery, there was a pit of dread that there would be no striving, no consciousness, no feeling, no nothing.

Maybe, that sensation was only an instinct to hold on until the tumultuous end. Was it just an autonomic response to the unknown or to what we do know? We are, after all, the only species aware of our own impending death. As far as I know. Wouldn't it be better not to know?

What I was feeling: like cold water slipping through my fingers.

The other way of looking at it, there would be relief when it was all over. Gone would be the unrelenting weight of disgrace pressing down on me. I wouldn't know I was gone because I would be gone. I wouldn't notice the absence of shame. I wouldn't miss the suffocation of my encompassing minor notoriety, bonded to me like Krazy Glue online, trailing after me wherever I ventured. I certainly wouldn't miss my banishment from the vacuity of my apartment. I'd be glad to be rid of the bustling solitude of the city. There'd be no remorse in the departure of the end of hope.

Good riddance to petty people, the trap of automated customer service, advertisements in elevated decibels for things I didn't know I needed, static electricity from the unnecessary folding of laundry, talking heads on TV talking about nothing with the import of everything, the yearnings of an untamed heart.

Distant and shallow breathing began to overcome me.

Last remembrances: I'd miss the rainbows in puddles I stepped over at the curb of sidewalks. A burst of extract, like fireworks, from a bite of a freshly baked cookie. The refrain of vulnerable honesty in a melody heard. The crescent moon in a clear night sky. The last of the drive-in movie theaters discovered on long-lost road trips. Childlike joy over silly things that don't matter like . . .

Like nothing.

None of it was enough.

Not nearly.

I wondered how much of the loosening of the moorings was a matter of choice, whether I could will myself to the bitter end, or did I need to continue ladling the little white orbs down my gullet?

I wasn't giving up so much as easing up on the reins, or so I sought to convince myself. *Stop resisting. Don't fight so hard.*

My heartbeat slowed.

I felt the verging.

I felt nothing.

"Look."

The voice. Again. I strained to open my eyes. That voice wasn't me. I was sure of it this time. I hadn't said anything. And, look at what? What was there to look at? What was I supposed to look at?

I strained to lift myself onto my elbows. I didn't see anything.

Why wouldn't the whispered word leave me alone? What was the point?

Was I just hearing things?

This was a first. Never before had I heard a voice speak to me—a voice without a body, a voice present but not, unseen but here, ephemeral but real.

But then again, why all the fuss? People heard voices all the time, didn't they? Joan of Arc, for one. But that was a long time ago, learned in a history book, and I didn't quite remember the details.

Who had spoken to her?

My verdict: Not important. A myth, no doubt. I'm sure

others could attest to the authenticity of whispered voices heard if not imagined.

Scanning the emptiness, I took in the blurry shapes before me, discounting one thing after another, dismissing the material objects seen—a toaster, balled socks—until my gaze came to a halt on the still image of the laptop resting on the rickety card table. A mirage? A monument to our postmodern times? A paperweight? The computer seemed to be beckoning me, but without words.

Definitely no words.

Not a single one.

# 3

It's a good thing no one was looking. It would've been hard to explain: I was crawling on all fours from the futon to the card table. There's no other way I could have bridged the distance of a mere three feet or so. I was upside down and inside out, dizzy to the point of not being sure I was actually present.

Another batch of pills would have to wait. The booze too. Not to mention the end.

On hold.

Trying not to throw up, I lunged at the foldup chair, clutching the backrest for balance—for a lifeline—pulling myself up to a half-standing position, more hunched, apelike, than *homo sapiens* erect. But it would suffice, as I pulled the chair out from beneath the table and plunked myself onto the hard metal seat.

Holding the edges of the table, I peered down at the silent laptop.

Vertigo struck. Swaying, I flipped the computer open, pressed the "on" button, and the contraption came to life, casting a ghost-like glow over the dim room now bathed in predawn shadows of unspent dreams.

Hour number three since the bar. Why was I still keeping track? A bad habit. Strapped to my right wrist was a superfluous watch, a monitor of the fractional passage of time, an anachronism of the twenty-first century, an accoutrement, jewelry marking clicks into the similitude of reality.

I knew the drill. I'd done this a million times in my other life as an investigative reporter: Find a person based only on one identifier or two. A name, a place, that was sufficient to get me on my way. I googled the Oklahoma Department of Corrections. Then I navigated to the inmate database and inserted the name—*what was it again?*—into the blank search field. A six-digit prisoner number popped up. I clicked on the blue hyperlink, and there she was.

Maggie.

Not what I expected. The photo staring back at me was that of a kid—not an adult—with hollow cheeks and a trace in the frozen eyes of something unmistakable: a testimony to agony, to deep despair.

Greetings, *mon amie.*

It was one of six photos. I clicked on the next. In this one, Maggie was a little older, as told by the filling out of her cheeks. Nourished. Color had returned to her face, yet it was inscrutable. Not happy. Nor sad. Just set, staring blankly, being there.

Then the next photo: Here, a little older, she was wearing glasses. Almost looked bookish. With longer hair, grown out. There was a subtle sense of growing confidence in her eyes, as if maturing into adulthood, beginning to understand who she was. Maybe I was reading too much into the braille of her morphing features.

The fourth photo: A hardening around the mirthless eyes, older still. The work of institutionalization, of hard times and harder experiences. An educated guess: By this point, Maggie had seen it all, and it wasn't good.

The fifth: This photo must've been more recent. There was a symmetry to her fine features, the crystalline of her emerald eyes, now easy in the way they peered into the unseen camera, as if acknowledging the admiration of the lens. It wasn't just that, though. She had somehow blossomed inside prison, like an unlikely wild daisy sprouting up in neglect between cracked asphalt plates.

There's that word again: Neglect.

And the sixth, the most recent snapshot: A smile—yes, she was actually smiling for the first time. What was she smiling about?

It wasn't just a throwaway smile, either. It seemed genuine. It was, I had to admit, a nice smile. No. Not nice. Didn't like nice. Nice didn't capture it. Nice shouldn't have been in my lexicon, not as a writer. Nice was coasting in neutral, safe, sanitized.

Maggie's smile was . . . incandescent.

Okay, fine. It wasn't just the smile. I'd admit, she also had a pretty . . . nose. Maybe it wasn't just the nose either. I mean, how do we explain these things? The things we instantly feel that are not contained in what is observed? The sum is greater than its parts, or something like that. Or maybe it goes back to childhood, a connection to what is familial—familiar if forgotten.

Wait. What was that? There was something about her eyes. How could they say so much without saying anything? A deep well of an elusive emotion, inviting, beckoning. They were shaped just so, sparkling, soft, iridescent.

Mascara?

Maggie was wearing makeup. A hint of paint around the eyes. How was that possible? Makeup wasn't issued in prison. Forbidden. Contraband. But then I remembered. In my work as an investigative reporter, other inmates had told me. They eked ink out of ballpoint pens into a fine mist, mixed it with a dab of water, heated the brew against a barely functional radiator, and—presto—applied to the face. Speaking of which. Maggie's face. Whether she'd meant to or not, she retained a wisp of innocence about her, a kind of wholesomeness in defiance of the stern place where she was warehoused. Was it the sprinkle of freckles on her cheeks—or something else? It was as if she kept a part of herself guarded against the invasion of prison with its shuttered inhumanity, the way the walls pressed unending days against the psyche.

I mumbled to myself: "She doesn't belong there."

Did I say that out loud? These were just pictures on a laptop. One dimensional. The pharmacological effects of the pills were speaking. The tequila was carrying me away. Actually, it was the other way around. The swaying was dissipating. The seasickness was abating. Alertness was returning, which was when I caught sight of the odd identifier in the corner of the computer screen above her picture:

## DOB: NOVEMBER 11, 1990

November 11. It was the same date as the discarded newspaper from the garbage can I had visited just hours earlier: 11/11. More symmetry. More concurrence. What did it mean? Nothing. A fluke. That's what I muttered: "Fluke." This time I was sure I uttered the word aloud.

What's more, before I get carried away, Maggie was born in 1990—not the year printed on the pages of the tabloid, 2011. Big difference. So there. Not really all that similar. And lest it be overlooked, we can find similarity where we want, if we try hard enough, if we seek internal logic where there is none. Let's face it: It's more comforting to believe there's a reason for everything—the good and the bad—that we are reigned by cause and effect, and that righteousness will be rewarded. It doesn't work that way. I was living proof, exhibit number one. Not that it was worth examining me. Not that it was necessary. I knew what was there without the benefit of reflection. A wreck. Hadn't shaved in—well, since the implosion. A biblical beard overtook practically half my face: incognito. Unrecognizable. Another person. I hadn't bothered to brush my hair, a tangle of vectors pointing in different directions, a look of studied disinterest. I had stopped going to the gym. Stopped answering my phone. Let the voicemails pile up until there was no more room. Ignored the emails. Half was junk anyway, solicitations for sundry services and fortunes left in the wills of wealthy people who didn't exist. Slept fitfully during the day. Stayed up restlessly at night. Immunized myself with drink. Dulled the senses with pills. Tried not to think. Didn't read. Wouldn't watch TV. Wrestled with the dark void, with myself, that miserable troglodyte howling on a deserted island of despair.

I was not exactly in a position to do much of anything, let alone help a prisoner in need. I couldn't even pick up the phone and call her. Prison didn't work that way. Besides, she didn't know I existed. Which was for the best. Maggie could do better. Much better. I needed to mind my own business. Deal with my own stuff. Tend to my issues. Confront my own devolvement, if I could ever find the reckless ambition. What else could I do anyway?

# 4

Dear Maggie,

Forgive me. I'm not sure where to start. Is there really a beginning, anyway? Or an ending? I'll just start in the middle, if you don't mind. I'm an investigative reporter—well, I used to be. In the name of full disclosure, I lost my job at the *Herald* recently. It's a pathetic long story that I won't inflict on you. But I'd completely understand if you decide not to read any further and toss this letter into the scrap heap.

You still there?

Okay. Here goes. Four hours ago this evening, I came across your case by accident, and the thing is, I think I might be able to help you. I've investigated a number of criminal cases. Actually, I should say it's a long shot. These things are always unlikely—that is, being freed from a wrongful conviction before your time is up. Just my opinion, but the system isn't designed to undo mistakes.

Sorry. I'm getting ahead of myself. Let me back up. I've

only read an old news brief about your case. But it left me with a bunch of questions. I'll try to familiarize myself with your case by requesting police records, 911 transcripts, and other public documents under the Freedom of Information Act. It's called a FOIA request. Maybe you've heard of the forms. I've drafted them before. So, I know what to do. But could you fill me in otherwise?

If you have them, the trial transcript and medical records would be helpful. Also, could you provide an account of the events that led to your arrest, to the best of your recollection? Please try not to leave out details. They sometimes make all the difference. And please provide the names and contact information of others who might know something about what happened a decade ago.

There's not much else to say, except this: I'm from New York City, which should tell you a lot. Not all good.

Well, that's all for now.

Sincerely,
Joe

P.S. Hope to hear back from you.

# 5

What was I thinking?

I wasn't. But nothing could be done. I had sent the letter, it was already wending its way through the postal system, to—what was that place called? Mabel Bassett Correctional Center on Kickapoo Road.

Idiot. Me. Not the place. Maybe the place. Didn't know. Not yet.

After flagellating myself for my headlong dive into a complete stranger's private affairs—an inmate who surely had better things to do than hear from a ruined investigative reporter—I resolved to forget the whole thing, wash it from my mind for good, never to revisit the topic for as long as I should live, so help me. Because. I had other stuff to do, important things, like fetching my dry cleaning. When the destruction occurred, I had left a white button-down shirt at the cleaners. Wouldn't need that costume anymore ever again. Not in this lifetime. But. Who knew? A white button-down shirt might come in handy if I was invited to, say, attend a funeral.

Maybe even my own.

Then again, I'd probably wear a ratty T-shirt for that festive occasion. Why get all dressed up for my own party? It'd be one of the few times—and the last—where I'd get to call the shots.

The prerogative of the dearly departed.

The preoccupation with death wouldn't leave me. Couldn't shake it.

Oh, and another thing. I needed floss. Had run out. Add it to the list. In addition to the dry cleaning. So there. Plenty to do. Things to attend to. Places to go to. First among them: a walk. To nowhere. Hands stuffed in jeans pockets. Head down. I wasn't really looking at anything, barely paying attention to the steep steps down to Riverside Park, the site of distant memories, happier days.

As I entered the park, the peal of laughter filled the sweltering air, past and present. A bunch of children danced joyously around a skittering sprinkler in a fenced playground. Couldn't shut it out. We were all once a small number, of a little age, even me. Where does it all go wrong? At what point do we lose that innocence? How does it go away? I say it doesn't happen at once. It's a slow erosion, invisible to the naked eye. And before you know it, the jungle gym becomes the jungle of Darwinian struggle, and the claws come out, ready to rip to death.

An unrelated thought intruded: I hadn't even bothered to ask Maggie the most important question of all. Was she guilty or innocent?

Didn't have the bravado to broach the subject, indelicate as it was. I was losing my reporter's edge. In the old days—just months earlier, before the ruination—I didn't hesitate to ask the impolitic question: How old are you? How much do you make? Did you kill the dog?

It was an occupational hazard, the stark directness. There was no such thing as small talk. Never one of my specialties, anyway.

A park bench. Fatigued from nothing, I plopped down a safe distance from all other humanity and allowed my perspective to meander from the sprinkler just yonder to the playful trot of pigeons seeking crumbs.

Overlooked was the absurdity of the attempt. Aside from my own ruination, how was I supposed to investigate a case with no witnesses, except apparently the accused herself? How was I supposed to look into an old case where there was little forensic evidence? There was no crime scene to speak of, nothing tangible to probe, other than a crib in what might've been a trap house.

Day rumbled into night, which churned into day again, and so it went, day after day, light and dark metastasizing into hues of metallic gray, blending indistinguishably into each other until I found myself back in the box of my sterile apartment, scrunched at the card table, contemplating a thick instruction booklet over a pile of Lego pieces. I was building an elaborate medieval castle with embattlements and escutcheons galore.

Just because. I wouldn't hear back, anyway. I'm sure she was busy. Prison classes. They could stretch for days, weeks even, or so I'd heard. There were the counts, too. Commissary. Let's not forget the indiscreet disclosure of my lack of a job, a hint of

my ruination. *Hope to hear back.* I wouldn't write back either.
Lunatic.

Back to Lego. Where was that piece? Sifting through the
rubble of Lego rectangles and squares and rubber tires, I couldn't
release the uneasy feeling I was missing a crucial piece.

Besides, it was futile. Maggie's case, that is.

*Ah, there it is.* A Lego piece in the shape of a circle with axles.
*What in the world was that for?*

But then again, I suppose it wouldn't do any harm if I
simply filled out the FOIA request, the request for public
records in Maggie's case. Even if I never heard back from her.
The Lego could wait. And nobody said I couldn't just submit a
FOIA request. I mean, why couldn't I just do it anyway?

Part of me wanted to know. The part that wasn't dead to
the world yet. Who knew what it'd yield? The police reports
could contain some whoppers. Same with the 911 transcripts.
Wouldn't be the first time. Might not hear back at all. From
the police, that is. Nor Maggie. Or from either.

Okay. Fine. I swiped the Lego pieces aside, the better to make
room for my incomplete thoughts. Reopened the laptop. Pulled
up the web page for Skiatook police. Found the FOIA form
online. What was the harm? I could simply ask for the old police
records in Maggie's case. What in the world could come of it?
Probably nothing. Just a shot in the pitch dark, aimed at nothing.

29

# 6

Dear Joe,

I have to make a confession. It was the strangest thing getting your letter. I was surprised that I wasn't surprised. It was like I was expecting to hear from you. Not you in particular. But someone. I've always held on to hope. When you've been stuck in a place like this for ten years with another ten to go, that's the only way to keep going. You've got to believe.

Every now and then, I look out a small window and I can see the parking lot just beyond the perimeter. Visitors come and go, mothers, fathers, and children. They hold plastic bags full of coins for the vending machines here. That's all they're allowed to bring in with them. Quarters. Money to buy pizza and cheeseburgers and Dr. Pepper. But I can never get to that parking lot. I'm surrounded by barbed wire, high walls, and gates. I'm shut in. I still have trouble getting my mind wrapped around that idea.

A good friend of mine on the inside just passed away. She got a bad diagnosis. It was cancer. But I figured she'd be okay. Then suddenly she was gone, like she never existed. Plain vanished.

That's how things work. Life just goes along, as they say in the pod here.

Anyway, if you want to hear my story, the first thing you'll want to know is that tragedy has always followed me like a long shadow. I never met my father. He died in a car crash when I was still in my mama's belly. I don't know much about him. I heard he was a tall drink of water, kind of like me. I was also told I inherited his toes, like long fingers.

Well, I suppose I should get straight to the point. What happened ten years ago stays with me like a homemade tattoo burned into my brain. I remember it better than what went down in the yard yesterday. I remember the way the stars lit up the sky that night. I remember the scent of freshly cut grass in the hills of Skiatook.

I was working at a little bar in town, pouring jack and tap. It was a job. It paid the rent, no thanks to my ex. His name is Ram. It's not his real name. That's what everyone called him. Something to do with his Native American background. It fits, the name. You'd have to know him to understand what I mean. Anyway, when I got home, it was after midnight, and Ram was dead to the world, snoozing on the recliner. That's how it was with him.

Our baby girl, Mary, was three months old and resting in the crib. I went to check on her, and she cried out. Something was wrong. I could tell right away. It wasn't her cry. It was something else. It was her eyes. They looked blank. I waved a finger in front of her but her eyes didn't track it.

I called out to Ram and told him something wasn't right with our baby girl. Ram rustled awake and mumbled something about not worrying about it. But I told him I was going to take Mary to the ER. Ram sat up groggy and said—I'll never forget this—"What if we get accused of child abuse?" I didn't give it any thought then.

All I knew was, I needed to get my baby girl to the hospital as soon as possible. I asked Ram if he was coming. He said no. There was no time to argue. I grabbed my things, took off, and the next thing I knew, I was being questioned at the hospital first by nurses, then doctors, then social services, and the cops.

I never got to see my Mary again. Social services took her away that night. I wasn't a mother anymore.

I don't know how many days passed but I sat in a county jail, wanting nothing but to kill myself. I refused to eat. I couldn't sleep. I didn't talk. It was like I was strangling on grief.

I didn't hear from my ex. Somehow, my mama scraped up enough money to get me released on bond. I think it helped that I didn't have any priors. Kept the bond down. When I came home, the apartment was empty and Ram was gone, which was just as well.

Sometimes, I'd imagine the whole thing was a bad dream and I'd wake up and fix up Mary's room, straightening out her crib, the stuffed animals, and the little teddy bear, her favorite. I'd think she'd be back any minute. It was like playing house.

When the trial started, there was all kinds of legal lingo,

and I didn't know what my attorney was doing. He was a public defender. He called no witnesses, except Ram, who showed up all cleaned up. I barely recognized my ex. Ram never got charged with anything. But he testified he didn't believe I would do anything to hurt our little girl. It was the last time I heard from him.

My attorney called no medical experts. I couldn't afford any, even though the whole case was medical. They labeled it "shaken baby syndrome." Had never heard such a thing. Mary had some bruises and what the doctors called a "subdural hematoma." I didn't even know what that fancy term meant until later. There was no way of seeing it but her brain was bleeding under the surface.

Whatever happened that night, my baby girl recovered. My attorney never got to mention that in court. The judge wouldn't allow it. I still don't know why. The jury never heard my baby got better. She's a healthy little girl. My attorney promised me he knew what he was doing. I trusted him.

The trial ended after three days, and the jury found me not guilty of the main charge, child abuse. I don't know why they said it that way, "not guilty." Innocent is more like it. But then came the wrecking ball. I was found guilty of child neglect. I can't explain it. It makes no sense. I was absolved of hurting my child. The jury acquitted me. I was innocent. I am innocent. No one was ever found guilty of harming my little girl. But I was found guilty of neglect, like I didn't do enough to stop the abuse no one was ever convicted of. Nothing makes sense in this world.

I got punishment on top of punishment. It wasn't just

that I got sent away for a stretch of twenty years. I lost my Mary. I lost my life. I was practically a child myself. I was twenty-one years old.

That's pretty much it.

There I go complaining. I guess I should mention it could be worse. What I mean is, it's not so bad in here. I've only been in three fights and knocked out twice. I keep to myself for the most part. I don't have much in the way of friends. But I try to make use of my time. That's all I have. I crochet. I scrapbook. I read a lot of scandalous romance novels. I reckon it's the one guilty pleasure I'm allowed. I pray. Jesus is with me.

Now you know everything. Well, not everything. I suppose you might want to speak with my mama. I've enclosed her contact information on a separate sheet of paper in the envelope with this letter. Better yet, you might want to visit her. She's not as scary as she might seem at first. You might learn something about the case if you talk with her. I should mention, Skiatook is a strange place. You'll see what I mean if you go there.

Blessings,
Maggie

P.S. Please write back.

# 7

My first thought: She's a Bible thumper. Not my thing. Not remotely.

Second thought: Things could be worse. Look at Maggie's situation. Much worse. She was eerily nonchalant about having gotten into three fights and being beaten unconscious *twice*, as if that was the limit before it got bad—two, not three. That's where she would've drawn the line.

I'd never been knocked out, except by myself, via the gentle pathway of drink and prescription drugs. And here I was, in a prison of my own making, my poor excuse of a life on the edge of a nuisance.

Third thought: We had some things in common, Maggie and I, an indescribable agony asking only for it to end, all of it. Let's leave that one alone. I was nothing if not an expert at avoidance.

Last thought: Maybe there was something there. I mean, about Maggie's case. She had no priors; this was her first conviction. She had maintained her innocence all along. She hadn't even been home in the preceding hours directly before her daughter, Mary, became unresponsive. That was easy enough to confirm from police reports. That was also easy enough for harm to have come to her little girl long before Maggie ever got home from pouring Jack Daniels at the bar. All kinds of mischief might've occurred before she got home: several hours' worth. And what of her ex's alleged statement? "What if we get accused of child abuse?" If Ram really said as much, that seemed like a red flag, at a minimum. Maybe even inculpatory. *Who says that in the heat of a medical emergency?* Why would he have said that—unless perhaps he had reason to be worried about his own actions? Why didn't he go with Maggie to the ER? This was his daughter, too. Wasn't his behavior a bit strange? Even troubling?

I stared out of a window at nothing in particular. Here, though, was another set of troubling questions: What was I going to do about it? Was I really going to just drop everything, whatever *that* was, and hop on an airplane to—where was Skiatook?—some place not far from Tulsa, Oklahoma? As if I was in the proper condition—the right frame of mind—to do anything effectively? When I could barely afford my regular diet of ramen noodles in a Styrofoam cup? But then it came again. The voice.

"Go."

That's all it said. Just once. In such a low whispered voice, I almost missed it, almost didn't hear the hushed directive, almost dismissed it. Thought I had maybe dreamed it. Then realized I hadn't. It wouldn't leave me alone. I couldn't erase the quiet invocation.

It could've been the effects of the drink. Or the drugs. Or a combination. But go *where?* Maybe it was telling me to go somewhere else. To go to sleep. To go to the park. To go to pot. Actually, I was already there, deleterious to the nth degree. But it kept coming to me to the point that, I'll readily admit, I reacted impulsively, without premeditation, a rash decision of a fool, which is why, in a matter of hours, I found myself flying thirty thousand feet above sea level, hovering over a layer of clouds stitched together in a featherbed, fetching the flight attendant, ordering a third plastic cup of double scotch on the rocks.

# 8

By the time I found my bearings, I was hunched at the wheel of a Dodge rental sedan, wending my way through suburban Tulsa traffic.

The unreality of the situation struck me: how this single day felt like a year compared to the prior days that blended into each other in stingy brevity. Maybe time was relative after all.

I'd replaced static agony with elemental action. I was doing *something*. It struck me as heightened reality, even the small things: the sights and sounds and hues of my surroundings. Everything was new, experienced for the first time, unsealed, and peeled back, causing me to pay special attention. I was walking and talking and moving like a newborn, uncertain, teetering in my mind. It was all unfamiliar, the terrain, the wide-open sky, the habits and culture of Oklahoma, as evidenced once I ignored the GPS and, with a few minutes to spare, stopped at a local place called Braum's for something to eat. I was famished from taking in all the new stimuli.

The young store clerk was polite to the point of near chipperness, and the attitude wasn't forced. In New York, you were usually met with sullen abuse from someone behind the counter who made you feel like you owed them for bothering to make an order. I mumbled unobtrusively for a small soft-serve ice cream swirl and justified it based on the nutritional value of the yogurt content. It'd be the healthiest thing I'd eaten in weeks.

As I moved, ice cream in hand, to sit at a table bolted to the floor, I passed a weathered man in a cowboy hat who nodded amiably at me. Caught off guard, I nodded back uncertainly. A friendly exchange between strangers never happens in my hostile urban sliver of the universe, unless it's instigated by a huckster with no good on his mind.

Consuming the ice cream, I tried to mind my own business, as was the custom from where I came, but a glance from someone sitting at a table facing mine caught my eye. She must've been a good twenty years older than I was, maybe more. She'd done up her hair just so, and I could see she was meticulously dressed in a blouse, designer jeans, and strappy high heels, one of which was dangling back and forth like a metronome. I couldn't help but admire her. She hadn't given in to the weight of time. She exuded a confidence and a pluck I hadn't seen much in my utilitarian environs, which were stripped of adornment and treacle postures. I could think this without being troubled. She smiled at me, beaming. I made an effort to volley a smile back, though it didn't come naturally. It came out more like a grimace.

That's it. Just a passing acknowledgment.

There was something freeing in the anonymity, of being in a foreign place, unknown to anyone, released from the ignominy of my recent past. I could be anyone—or no one—it didn't matter either way. I could just go about my way, undisturbed by fact or circumstance. I could even breathe in the air, growing fragrant, as I navigated beyond Tulsan suburbia into the countryside, past little towns full of antique stores and coffee shops not owned by big box chains, cutting deeper into an array of untended fields, pockets of peaceful solitude, modest farms and ranches, an expanse of quiet beauty intermingled with abandoned stripped vehicles, including a rusted-out truck without wheels perched on cinderblocks.

As I neared my destination, the GPS in the rental got confused. I'd been warned this would happen. GPS had run out of digital maps. I was off the grid. The car didn't know where I was. These were uncharted lanes, rough roads carved out of cowboy country, some without names. I'd have to go old school, resorting to a paper map. Even that I found mildly quaint as I squinted at the crisscross of multicolored lines guiding me to the endpoint, deep in the backroads of Skiatook. What kind of name was that, anyway? What did it mean? I mouthed the strange word: "*Skiatook*."

What was I doing here? Was I really here? Was any of this occurring?

Probably of Native American origin, the town. That's what it sounded like to me, the Yankee interloper. Nothing like New York. The opposite. High rises were replaced by towering trees. No idea what kind. Only had a passing familiarity with foliage and such. Concrete and steel—now those I could spot-check routinely. But horses and wide-open spaces—they were as exotic to me as a chimera from a romantic land of imagination. Lot of stuff going on in Oklahoma, a subtext of forgotten Native American history and influence in passed highway signs: Broken Arrow. Osage. Shawnee. A complicated history, no doubt, comprised of bloodshed and the forced removal of indigenous people from their lands, the American shame. But I didn't know the story, not really.

I pulled into a muddy driveway and parked. An aproned figure stood, arms folded tightly, on a sun-scorched porch. Maggie's mama, no doubt.

# 9

Maggie's mama had been expecting my arrival in Skiatook. I'd spoken with her by phone from New York ever so briefly. She had been monosyllabic, with a bitter drawl. Yes. No. Right. Fine. Now, she was holding an egg timer. "You're late, mister," she noted, eyes narrowed. At least she had graduated to polysyllabic utterances.

"My apologies, ma'am," I said as I climbed out of the Dodge rental, second-guessing the whole soft-serve ice cream diversion.

Not sure why I said Ma'am. Never said that. Wasn't part of my vocabulary. Didn't fit in the confines of New York City. I was already pantomiming politeness.

"You have forty-five minutes," she said, displaying the egg timer.

"Forty-five minutes?"

"Until I've gotta fetch an apple pie from the oven," she said, and summarily turned her back to me, slamming a screen door behind her.

I took the gesture to mean I ought to follow her into the house, which I did, easing the screen door shut so it didn't slam with a racket. In the dim light, I could see Maggie's mama was already sitting at the wooden kitchen table, along with her egg timer, which was clicking away impatiently, in beat with the tapping of her index finger.

"Mind if I sit?" I asked politely.

"Go ahead," she said, sounding like she *did* mind.

"Thank you, ma'am." There I went again. I pulled out a reporter's pad and pen and took note of the stern visage before me. She had Maggie's nose. Or rather, the other way around; Maggie had her mama's nose. Crow's feet brought a severity to her glowering, unblinking eyes. She was boring a hole right through me to the other side of the kitchen. I glanced behind me. A country-style breakfront squatted there. On its shelves sat a collection of porcelain angels in various poses of prayer. Maybe this is where Maggie got it from, her faith.

"What do you want?" Maggie's mama asked without preliminaries.

"Sorry?" I replied, slightly taken aback. Had she already googled me? Did she already know of my ruin? Was I already discounted?

Even more, had she already figured me out? That I'd taken a peek at pictures of her daughter on the Department of Corrections inmate search website, causing a shift in the tectonic plates? That the tone and loops in the handwritten words of Maggie's letter had tugged at something unspoken but felt?

"With my daughter Maggie," she said. "What do you want with her?"

To speak with her?

To meet her?

To see her?

Shifting uncomfortably in my chair, I said, "I want to help her."

Maggie's mama leaned back in her chair such that it creaked dubiously.

"Little late for that," she remarked. "Wouldn't you say?"

"Could be," I said. "Can't make any promises."

Boilerplate from other investigations: It's what I always said. Not just to the victims. But to my editors. Needed to lower expectations. Because you never knew. These things were never easy. Plans always went awry. People were unpredictable. You'd game the whole thing and map out the seven possible human reactions to a given situation, and it'd end up being an eighth you never considered. Because life was messy, investigations were hard, and fiction was more plausible than what happened in real life.

"Little late for promises," Maggie's mama said. "Don't trust them, anyway."

Thirty-seven minutes left on the egg timer. She looked impatient. Like the apple pie was beckoning her. The waft of homemade crust tingled the olfactory senses. I figured I better move along.

"The thing is," I said, searching for the right words, "I think Maggie may be innocent."

"Maggie's innocent all right," she shot back indignantly.

How dare I not be sure? "If you don't mind my asking," I pursued delicately, "how do you know?"

"I just know," she said, folding her arms conclusively.

I knew this: That this was the end of one line of questioning. "Understood, Ma'am," I said, wondering where to go next with my inquiry.

"Besides," she continued, "what difference does it make now?"

"Excuse me?" Hers seemed like an odd question.

"It's been ten long years," she said. "We've already appealed the trial and lost. There's nothing left. What can you do?"

It felt more like an indictment than a query. "I need to find evidence," I said.

"Evidence?"

"Something new," I explained. "A witness. A record. Physical evidence."

"What're you getting at?" She was leaning forward in her chair for the first time.

"If I find something exculpatory, if I find something that points to Maggie's innocence, she could petition for a new trial or . . ."

"Or?"

"Or file for post-conviction relief."

"Meaning what?"

"She has a chance of being set free."

Now Maggie's mama was paying no heed to that egg timer. While it ticked away, all she said was, "Is that so?"

"It's possible," I said, "but I don't want to get your hopes up."

More boilerplate. Like fine print, the product disclosure: Don't try this at home. It might not work. Probably won't.

Could lead to an unmitigated disaster of epic dimensions. Probably would.

"You've done this before?" She seemed to not take into account my caution, clinging to hope anyway.

"On occasion," I said. "But it's a bit like getting hit by lightning."

"Lightning?"

"It's pretty rare."

She stood up and fetched a glass of water for me. I'd been upgraded.

"Ever think about how all of this is biblical?" she asked, retaking her seat across from me.

"Sorry?" I had no idea what she was talking about.

"Jesus," she said, measuring my response.

"Yes?" I still had no clue.

"He was wrongfully convicted and crucified on the cross," she said.

"Yes, Ma'am." I didn't know what else to say.

"Joseph," she added.

"Yes?" I thought Maggie's mama was referring to me, even though everyone called me Joe, not Joseph, except my mother, to scold me, and she wasn't around anymore, except when she haunted my dreams.

"No, not you," Maggie's mama said. "You're *Joe*. I'm talking about *Joseph* of the Old Testament. You might've heard of him. He was falsely accused, too."

Being an unbelieving heathen, I didn't know who she was talking about.

"Thou shalt not bear false witness," she intoned. "You've heard of that?"

"One of the Ten Commandments," I offered tentatively. I'd seen the classic movie on rerun TV when I was a kid. I wasn't a complete ignoramus.

Maggie's mama let the commandment settle in before continuing.

"You sure you want to do this?" she asked, leaning forward at the kitchen table, pushing the egg timer aside.

"Ma'am?"

"You don't know what you're getting yourself into," she said with a trace of foreboding. "Things you don't know."

I wasn't aware I was sitting mutely for several beats, trying to take in what she said, before recovering. "What do you mean?"

"Don't know if you want to go fixing to get involved in other people's business," she said, though without aggression.

It occurred to me that's exactly what investigative reporting is—getting involved in other people's business, in a manner of speaking. The only difference here, I suppose, was that I was investigating without a plan to write anything about it like I had in my previous life at the *Herald*. No news outlet. I was on my own, a scribe no more, and I felt I should press her on what she meant about getting into other people's business. I sensed there was more to her point—not all good, by the way. What *didn't* I know? What was I getting myself into? What would I find digging in other people's business?

But she wasn't finished. "Why Maggie?" she asked.

"Excuse me?"

"Why do you want to help my daughter?" She was eyeing me warily. "I reckon there are a lot of folks out there needing assistance."

I looked down at the kitchen table. "I think she may be

innocent," I said, feeling like I was teetering on shaky ground, not unlike a thin sheet of ice about to break open underneath me.

"You said that already," she said. "About Maggie being innocent."

I glanced up. She hadn't unfastened her gaze on me. It wasn't a hostile look. At least not overtly. Then again, it wasn't *not* a hostile look. I was beginning to understand what Maggie meant when she said her mama wasn't as scary as she first seemed.

Wily was more like it. Like a fox. Maybe it was an Oklahoma thing.

"It can't be helped," I said haltingly.

As soon as the words escaped from my mouth—the passive voice, the use of vague language, gobbledygook—I realized I'd said too much, not thinking, and I feared the worst. This is what happens when I've been unmoored from humanity going on four weeks. I wasn't ready for a grilling from a country-smart mama with an intuitive radar. The egg timer chugged along. This might be the part where she throws me out the screen door, never to be seen again, banished into the wilderness, back to my withered self in the box.

Maggie's mama didn't move an iota. The apple pie would have to wait. The scent of—*what was that?*—cinnamon wafted like a sprinkle of pixie dust across the kitchen table. A pause stretched out longer than it should have. Neither of us moved, as if we were locked in a battle of who would blink first. Maggie's mama won.

"You always have that beard?" she asked.

It wasn't the question I expected, not nearly. On the surface, it seemed like a monumental digression, but something told me it wasn't, not the way she was surmising me, appraising the damage.

"No, ma'am," I said. "The beard's a pretty recent addition." Scrutinizing me, she pursed her lips. "I see."

I wondered whether she would mention the wild tangle of hair on my head next. I should've brushed my hair for the occasion. But she let it go. She was onto other matters of more import.

"You should know something," she said.

That worried me. If I should know something, it meant I didn't know it, even though I should have. And there was a lot I didn't know.

"You can't see Mary," she said.

"Oh?"

"Mary is Maggie's daughter," she clarified, though I knew who she was talking about. I just didn't know why. "Mary is ten years old now. Beautiful little girl, my granddaughter. Healthy as a horse, mind you. Mary's been adopted by my cousin, Martha."

"Okay," I said, still not seeing the point.

"And," she said, dripping with disdain, "Martha believes Maggie is guilty. Martha believes Maggie hurt Mary all those years ago." She swiped at the kitchen table as if removing crumbs, but there were none. The apple pie was still in the oven.

"Mary doesn't know her mother exists," she said. "She has no memory of Maggie. Mary thinks she was adopted, which she was. But not in the way that she knows. Cousin Martha's sworn me to secrecy."

Her statement, unexpected as it was, opened a novella of

questions but I refrained. Maggie's mama had more to say, I could see by the way she was wrestling with the idea of opening her mouth.

I said nothing. I seemed to be getting more by *not* asking questions. Had to go with that. Maybe that was an Oklahoma thing, too. If there was anything I had learned as an investigative reporter, it was to trust my instincts.

"You can't see Ram either," Maggie's mama said. "Maggie's ex. He's disappeared into thin air. A real winner. She really knew how to pick 'em."

"I see," I said, though I didn't.

"Turd," she said. "Excuse my French."

"What can I do then?" I asked. "I mean, about Maggie's case."

She turned her eyes upwards, as if searching for answers in the ceiling. "You can go to the bar where Maggie used to work," she suggested. "The place is called the Sooner Second. Just down the road."

"Okay," I said, noting that everything seemed to be just down the road without a postal address. "That's a start."

"But you won't get anything there."

"Why not?"

"You're an outsider," Maggie's mama said, peering at my ragged beard. "Locals will never talk to you."

The unchangeable condition of the investigative reporter. I was always the ultimate outsider, wherever I was, whether I was among the impersonal sentries of New York or here in the quaint country charm of Skiatook. I was always on the outside, trying to look in, trying to figure out what was what, where I was in the unfinished puzzle, the shape of which I couldn't gauge.

"Fair enough," I said.

"But," she said, perking up at a new thought, "you can go to the gravesite."

"The gravesite?"

"That's where Maggie's father is buried," she said, folding her hands neatly before her.

"Your husband?"

"We were never married," Maggie's mama said, almost cracking a smile but not quite. "Like mother, like daughter. We aren't the marrying kind."

I let that go. "What could I learn at the gravesite?" I asked, trying not to sound disrespectful.

"Who knows?" Maggie's mama shrugged noncommittally. "Maybe nothing."

The egg timer dinged.

# 10

Maggie's mama was right. I didn't get anything out of the bar, except unwelcoming stares. When I arrived at the old graveyard, there was nothing there either. All I could see were rows of headstones in every direction, sheltered under wilting boughs.

What was I doing here anyway? But then I answered my own question. In investigations, you start on the outside and work your way in. You hunt down the leads in front of you, even the far-fetched ones. Because you never knew. There could be something.

For all the somnolent death surrounding me, this undisturbed reserve for the departed was teeming with wildlife. Chicks chirped in nests woven into the gnarled branches above me. Squirrels scurried about, gathering sustenance. Above, a squadron of birds in V formation soared toward the horizon, mimicked below by the spread wings of a single jet-engine airplane.

Can we only create from what we observe?

More to the point: Were those graceful creatures in the sky geese, swans, or ducks? Add that question to my lack of knowledge about the nature of trees. The closest thing resembling the animal kingdom in New York City came in the form of jostling pedestrians on Fifth Avenue carrying bags of overpriced merchandise.

As I picked my way through stone grave markers, seeking Maggie's father's, I kept envisioning my own. The epitaph in my mind mocked me:

BELOVED BY ONE, MAYBE
REMEMBERED BY NONE
UNFINISHED
UNDONE

Scoffing, I derided myself for my congenital inability to come up with a better ending. Even the stone tablet at my final resting place lacked proper phraseology. The inscription needed editing.

But imagining the rest, I'd be intermingled with earth in a decomposing box. Another box. A smaller box. A better box. Ineffectuality was enhanced by futility. I couldn't find Maggie's father's headstone, and I was about to abandon the effort when—for a fleeting moment—I thought I caught sight of a phantom.

An emaciated old man. I think. With a shock of white hair. At the mossy edge of the cemetery. But when I took another look, it—he—was gone. Had I imagined that? A gossamer of my own creation?

I couldn't say for sure.

All I could do was tell Maggie about it in a subsequent letter.

Maybe she would know what to make of it. This, after all, was her old stomping grounds. It wasn't lost on me that she had mentioned in her letter that Skiatook was an odd place. Or strange.

Aren't they the same thing?

In the postscript to my next letter, I mentioned to Maggie a funny feeling that remained with me even after my return to New York. I had a sense that, for all the dead ends I encountered during my trip to Skiatook, I had missed something—something there but unseen.

# 11

Dear Joe,

I wish I could tell you more but I'm not sure what you saw at the cemetery. It could have been anyone, even my dead father haunting you, for all I know. Like I said, Skiatook is a strange place.

All I can tell you for sure is I was glad to get your last letter. In this place, it's easy to be forgotten. It happens to everyone if you're here long enough. After a while, the visits slow down until they stop dead in their tracks. Even the letters trickle to just about nothing. Before you know it, your best friend is someone you just met who got pulled off the streets for some crime she won't talk about and now she's bunking next to you, snoring like a banshee.

Let me tell you another thing you don't know. My father died in a head-on car crash with an 18-wheeler. He was killed on impact while he was sitting in the passenger seat of a Toyota. His best friend was driving the car late that night. He fell asleep at the wheel. Somehow, he survived the wreck. Name of Enos. He still lives in a shack down by the junkyard in Skiatook. But Enos won't breathe a word about what happened that night. Never has.

The only thing my mama learned was what she got out of authorities when she collected my father's remains. They told her that another car—his own pickup—was found at the tip of Texas on the border with Mexico in some kind of resort town called South Padre Island.

My father's truck was parked by a pier overlooking barrier islands in the Gulf of Mexico. The vehicle looked immaculate, like someone had cleaned it top to bottom and inside and out. I have no idea what my father's pickup was doing down there. I have no idea why he left it there. I don't have any idea why his truck had been wiped down looking brand new. I mean, he was sitting in the passenger seat of his best friend's Toyota, right?

I know what you're thinking. Those Texas border towns are notorious for drug runners coming up from the Mexican cartels. I've heard the scuttlebutt, especially where I am now. I suppose there could be a connection to my father's death. But there I go again off-topic. What happened to my father has nothing to do with my case. I just figured you'd want to know since you paid a visit to the gravesite. Anyway, that's all for now.

Blessings,
Maggie

P.S. My mama told me you weren't "too bad." Coming from her, that's a pretty high compliment :)

# 12

There was, perhaps, only one other person on the face of the planet who still might have thought I wasn't too bad, besides Maggie's mama: Tally. My little sister—who wasn't so little anymore—was the only person I was pretty sure would show up at my funeral if—when—it came to that anticipated day.

"Joe."

"What?" I said, looking up.

"Did you hear what I said?"

There was a spoonful of apple sauce suspended in midair. Tally was the holder of the utensil, and she appeared slightly more perturbed than Abby, her infant daughter, who was sitting in a highchair, curls of soft hair wreathed around her cherubic face, awaiting the airplane landing of the apple sauce into her open mouth.

"Sure," I said morosely.

"What did I say?" Tally asked, frowning, calling my bluff.

"No idea," I said without remorse.

"You need to get over it," she said, ladling the spoon to its destination.

Tally was younger than I but she was always tougher and wiser. A single mother and corporate executive, she didn't have time for my congenital weaknesses. Environment or DNA? Nature or nurture?

"You need to get a life," she continued.

Was that the same thing as needing to get over it?

Tough love. That's probably what she would call this lecture. The old kick in the pants. The old put-on-your-big-boy-pants.

"People have short memories," she said.

I couldn't help but still think of Tally as a five-year-old, a rambunctious child with endless energy and a refusal to comply with any reasonable request unless it was attached to a bribe of candy. She was an accident, after my birth. A necessary accident. We didn't talk about such vital things. Personal history was best left untouched. Now here she was, in the dining room of her posh New York apartment, all stylish in capri pants and a blouse more reminiscent of our mother, may she rest in peace. Tally was so normal. Not ruined, for one. But it was more than that.

When did this happen?

Tally was multitasking, wiping apple sauce from her shoulder, while she volleyed verbal instructions at me; not sure how it got there—the apple sauce or the disquisition. She was removing Abby from her highchair. Tally was kicking some toys out of the way on the floor. She was checking her work email.

"The internet doesn't," I finally said, breaking my silence.

"The internet doesn't *what?*" Tally replied, pausing from the juggling act.

"The internet doesn't have a short memory," I said robotically. "It lives forever."

Tally peered dubiously over her shoulder at me on her way out of the dining room, child in tow. Some minutes later, when she returned empty-handed, she sat across the table from me, waiting.

"The internet follows you wherever you go," I said, resuming my diatribe.

"People don't keep track," she said, wiping her hands. "They have their own problems."

Now it was my turn to peer dubiously at Tally.

"Don't know what I'm doing here," I grumbled.

"I invited you," Tally said.

"Not what I meant."

"Fine. I ordered you to come here."

"Didn't mean that either," I said.

Tally didn't ask me what I meant.

"I just can't get it out of my mind," I said in a flat tone. "How it could've happened. I keep playing it over and over in my mind. I can't help it. It just doesn't make sense. I had checked with my sources. I had multiple sources. The story was fact-checked. I went over everything. My editors had signed off on it."

Tally remained silent.

"I'm telling you, I'm *right*," I said, almost rousing myself to animation. "What I wrote was the truth."

Tally looked at me with sympathy, not unlike how a mother would gaze at a pouting child.

"Not that it matters anymore," I said, pulling myself together. "It all goes away so quickly, with the way social media works." Then I added for effect: "Cancel culture."

Tally nodded her head; this wasn't the time for placating platitudes.

"There's only one short-term solution," I said, rising from the table, ready to leave. "I need to move to a thatched hut on a remote tropical island where they don't have the internet or speak English."

# 13

Still here.

# 14

Dear Joe,

It's been a while since I heard from you so I figured I'd send a letter and say hi.

Hi.

Well, that's out of the way. I also realized I should've asked about you when I last wrote. Here I was going on all about my own problems and not stopping to have the decency to ask about yours. So, tell me all about them. And don't go saying you don't have problems. You already mentioned you lost your job. I get the feeling there's more to the story. Am I right?

My mama said the beard isn't you, whatever that means. (I think she thinks you'd be better off without it. But then again, I've never seen you and she's full of opinions if you hadn't noticed.)

What happened to you? I should warn you about something: When you've been where I've been for as long as I've been, you develop a radar for suffering. I can spot it a country mile away.

I should tell you one other thing: Whatever it is that ails you, it's going to be okay. What I mean is, God will make it right. God is always there. Here. Everywhere. You are never forgotten. You are made in His image. It may not make sense what you're going through, what you've been through, but there is always hope. There is purpose in pain. You just need to get to the other side.

One last thing: It's okay if there's nothing you can do for me. My case is old. I've already done near ten years. I know this place better than what's on the outside. I'm used to my routine. I wake up early. I pray. I go about my business. You start to get comfortable with it all. I find joy in the little things, things that can't be blocked out, not from the yard anyway, like a beautiful sunset when the sky lights up in colors you didn't think was possible. Burnt orange. Pink of a divine nature.

I find joy when I lose myself in the pages of a good book. There's happiness when a friend is set free. I'm a student in a cosmetology course here, and I've learned all about pedicures and manicures. You'd be surprised how complicated this stuff gets.

Here's another thing. I've grown up on the inside. It's what I've come to understand. I missed the whole smartphone revolution. Back in the day, before I came here, I had a flip phone, which was kind of like a Star Trek gadget. You'd flick your wrist to open up the phone and then you'd dial a number. That was about it. Nothing like today's fancy phones, which can talk back at you, even if you don't want them to. By the way, those smartphones are contraband here.

And forget about social media. None of that existed in my day, way back when. Thank goodness is what I say. I don't miss what I don't know.

So, I guess what I'm saying is, I can do the rest of my time. I know there's something out there for me ten years from now. One day, I hope to travel. I want to see Paris and Rome and Greece, all the places I've seen in books. In my mind, I can see the Parthenon. I can envision the Colosseum. I can picture myself at the top of the Eiffel Tower. I've never been anywhere other than Oklahoma, and I know there's a whole wide world out there.

My secret desire? To drive across America in an RV, a window open, the wind rushing through my hair. Ever see the world's largest ball of twine in Kansas? How about the Paper House in Massachusetts? I hear the mountains and waters of Lake Tahoe are something to behold. Is that in Nevada or California? Never get that straight.

Anyway, what I'm thinking is, I'd drive up the coast in an old RV, along California State Route 1, to Big Sur. I get the feeling that would be a good place to stop and take in the great wide ocean, the sky that goes on forever, and the beautiful majesty of God.

I know there is a purpose. I know there is a reason why I'm here. I accept it. The way I see it, it's simple. I'm halfway home.

Blessings,
Maggie

P.S. You ought to get yourself a dog.

# 15

A dog?

Where'd that come from? I could barely take care of myself, let alone a four-legged creature who would actually need to be walked every so often in all that lurking danger out there in the world. Among careening cars. Falling objects. Ordinary people.

And while we're at it, how did it get to the point where Maggie was comforting *me*? There she was, telling me in her letter that it would be all right. The nerve. Shouldn't it have been the other way around? Wasn't I supposed to be the one encouraging her? Wasn't she the one locked up in prison, not me? Why was she so maddeningly optimistic? Didn't she need a boost? I was on the outside. I could do whatever I wanted. I could go skydiving. I could climb the Adirondack mountains.

I could even do something as simple as buy a candy bar, which she couldn't do without a requisition form. Not that I'd ever buy that candy bar. More savory than sweet, that was me. But in theory . . . that was the point. Wasn't it?

And yet.

The hard truth was, Maggie was more resilient than I was. For all her suffering, for all that she had lost—her child, her freedom, her life—she was filled with a hope I didn't understand. On the inside, she was more free than I was on the outside. She let her mind roam. She could see a future. She didn't impose limits on what was possible. I did. For one, who was renting the RV? Figured there was no way she was buying one, not after prison. Those recreational vehicles cost a pretty penny, right?

Meanwhile, I was in my own form of solitary confinement, in my own stifling box, though not at the moment, because I found myself back in Skiatook, back to the case. I was down by the junkyard, knocking on the front door of the shack of Enos, who had survived the car crash that killed Maggie's father years ago. I didn't know if there was anyone on the other side of the door. I didn't know why I was back. Should've left well enough alone. Should've let it go. Maggie said as much.

The voice didn't even tell me to return to Skiatook. It was just what I told myself: Didn't have anything else to do. Maybe there was no point in this door knock. Wouldn't set Maggie free, that's for sure. Maybe all I'd do was find out what happened to Maggie's father. Maybe that would bring her some measure of closure, just to know. *Closure.* Hate that word. Too neat.

But curiosity was a congenital problem of mine.

Another problem: I didn't have an appointment. Wasn't expected. This was an unannounced house call, which used to be one of my specialties as an investigative reporter. Go forth and knock on the door of a source who doesn't know you're coming, who doesn't want to speak with you. In some cases, I'd been specifically warned not to come by. Harm would come to me if I did.

I always went anyway. Most of the time, I got in the door. They let me in. I was more charming back in the day. Actually, I couldn't congratulate myself too much. It was merely a matter of human nature. It is hard to turn someone away when they're looking straight at you, when you've come a long way to speak with them, when there's something important at stake. "No" is harder in person.

I knocked on the door again. It wasn't much of a door. The plywood shook from its inherent flimsiness. I could've easily ripped the door off the frame by its handle. Makeshift. Untended. Warped from neglect.

There was that word again: *neglect.*

I was about to turn away when the knob turned of its own accord, and the door creaked open enough for me to see, on the other side, an old man with a shock of white hair.

"How'd you find me?" he blurted out.

I didn't know I'd found anyone until he asked the question, and then, in a flash of an instant, I connected the dots, realizing I was facing the old man I'd spied at the cemetery on my last visit to Skiatook. It wasn't my fault he happened to be the same person who had followed me while I was in the cemetery searching for the headstone of Maggie's father. Now, I was just looking for Enos, the old friend of Maggie's father. What I had seen at the cemetery last time wasn't a ghost, after all.

"Enos?" I asked.

He didn't open the door any further. He didn't close it either.

"Didja follow me here?" Enos asked.

"No, sir," I said.

More politeness. That didn't quite solve the mystery of how I found him. But the agitation was evident in his dubious squint.

"Why'dja come here?" he asked.

"I'm helping Maggie," I said, thinking better of asking to be let in.

"Nothin' I can do about Maggie's case, tragic as it is," he said.

"I understand you were behind the wheel of the car when her father died in the crash."

That seemed to catch him by surprise. "You oughta let that alone, or—"

He stopped himself from betraying any more.

"—Or?" I asked.

"Or more people might die," he said, glancing behind me warily, as if searching for others.

"What people?" I asked.

"I've said too much already," he said, and slammed the door.

For a moment, I stood at the threshold, wondering what had just happened. Who might die? Me? Someone else? Who had died? Was Enos referring to Maggie's father, or was it another person—or persons? And why was the threat of death an issue after all this time, some thirty years after the car crash, assuming that was what he was referring to? Come to think of it, what had Enos been doing snooping around the cemetery, stalking me the last time I had visited Skiatook? And what, if anything, did the death of Maggie's father have to do with her own criminal case?

# 16

Sometimes, you have to be willing to fail spectacularly to achieve minor success. That's what I used to crow as an investigative reporter. Which was why I had booked another flight—what was another bothersome charge on the mountain of credit card debt?—and landed in Houston, where I picked up an economy rental and drove all the way down to the edge of the parched Mexican border.

There, I crossed the longest bridge I'd ever seen onto a sliver of lush tropical land caressed by the deep cobalt Gulf. A small sign, under pictures of multicolored umbrellas and coconut trees, greeted me: South Padre Island, Texas.

Well, now I was in it.

Feeling a bit like I'd just parachuted onto foreign terrain,

I did what I always did at first. I checked into a cheap motel, the kind where the clerk barely looks up when passing you the room key on a flimsy plastic fob that looks like a throwback to the 1950s. The room décor: hues of dingy dusty mauve.

Fancy words for dirty brown. My kind of poor palace.

Per habit from my days as an investigative reporter, when I was often followed, threatened, and attacked, I checked all the dark places—on the other side of the shower curtain, under the queen-sized bed, behind the calico-colored curtains. Nobody lurking anywhere.

Just me.

As was my custom, I placed the "Do Not Disturb" tag on the outside of the room door handle so as not to be bothered, whether I was in the room or not. And lastly, I turned on the TV just loud enough that it could be heard, in case anyone might want to know if anyone was inside when I wasn't. This wasn't paranoia; this was rational behavior based on experience.

The next thing I did was out of necessity. In the cramped motel bathroom, where there was barely enough room not to bump into myself, I showered, shaved off my wild beard, and brushed my tangled tuft of unruly hair. Didn't want to scare the island natives, especially when I'd be making a lot of inquiries about a strange occurrence from three decades ago. Needed to be presentable. Or at least hide my misery. That would be too much of a distraction.

It took some doing, and when I peered in the smoky mirror, I barely recognized myself. Who was *that* guy? Not me. I felt like a fugitive. There was an angularity I didn't recognize that had been hidden by the beard but was now exposed. The pupils of the eyes contained an ineffable anguish, wells of darkness. I couldn't sustain the appraisal; it was as if I was too shy to look back at the joyless person staring back at me from inside the mirror.

Too much reality.

But I suppose Maggie's mama would approve of the look, sans the beard. Speaking of which, I pulled out the frayed old photo of Maggie's father she'd lent to me. He looked too young to be gone. Not even a trace of worry lines. He was lanky, with a hitch in his pose. He was grinning crookedly, like he knew something you didn't and wasn't about to tell you. Like he didn't have a care in the world and it was all in front of him, the promise of a rollicking future of banditry.

The only other photo in my possession was of his truck, the one that was discovered after his death, parked by the pier down here on South Padre Island. The truck, more than thirty years later, looked like an antique, rounded at the edges with chrome accents. Not immaculate, as the vehicle was discovered abandoned. But sometime before that, in a neglected state of rust and caked mud.

*Neglected.* The word, in all its forms, wouldn't leave me alone.

All that was left for me to do was to put on the least offensive, most benign clothing I owned: a baby blue button-down and a pair of nondescript dungarees. I tucked in the shirttail. First impressions count in the act of investigating: what you wore, whether you got enough sleep the night before, the degree of the crease in your protractor smile.

Based on prior attempts, I knew I had three seconds—not an iota more—when I approached complete strangers before they made an instinctive decision: to speak with me or turn away.

With the ritual overtures out of the way, I ventured forth in the car rental feeling like I was a traveling encyclopedia salesman, except without the encyclopedias. When I steered to the ocean pier and parked, I began by walking against traffic.

Another reflex of my former investigative reporting days. The thinking was, it was safer to see cars coming toward you than from behind. Less likely to be caught by surprise, or pulled from behind, unawares, into a car, kidnapped, and taken to a secondary crime scene where worse things would happen. I'd seen too many crime scene photos.

Next, I needed to gird myself. I was shy by nature, unlike my little sister, Tally, who never had trouble filling a room with her unfiltered presence. Me, I preferred to recede into the background. I didn't need to accentuate myself. I was too much in my own headspace anyway, especially now. But I needed to be someone else. I needed to be the other me, the one who chatted with strangers with aplomb, the one who placed imaginary armor over myself, protection against awkwardness and constant rejection.

"Hi there," I began on entering an ice cream shop on the gulf side boardwalk, where the storefront sign proudly proclaimed it'd been in business since 1988. Before the car crash. There was a chance. The proprietor might've been around when Maggie's father parked his truck nearby decades ago.

"What can I do you for?" asked the chirpy young clerk behind the counter.

"Don't suppose there's anybody who works here who was around back in 1990?"

The clerk scratched the peach fuzz on his chin. "Can't help you there, buddy."

*Buddy.* Another one of my least favorites. I was bankrupt of buddies. And he sure hadn't earned that privilege of becoming one. I figured I better depart before I was tempted to smush Oreo cookie ice cream in his mug.

"Have a nice day!" he called out.

I let the door slam behind me without responding. Hated that, too—the word *nice,* along with the whole misbegotten phrase, to "have a nice day." It was all so cheerful. Out of context.

As it turned out, no one knew anything on this sweltering day. Not the florist. Not the dental hygienist. Not the T-shirt vendor. No one recognized the frayed photo of Maggie's father. No one had an inkling about any old immaculate truck parked by the pier a million years ago. And why in the world would they? Nobody even bothered to ask me who I was, whether I had an I.D., never mind that I was just some average Joe. A Joe Schmo.

My sales pitch only fetched bewildered looks. Some guy died in a car crash about thirty years ago. The crash didn't even occur anywhere near this island haven. Happened a couple of hundred miles away in a different vehicle, belonging to a guy named Enos, on Route 77 not far from Corpus Christi, which might as well have been another country. So why did the person in question, the victim of a car crash, leave his own truck behind at the pier here? Who cared that it was immaculate? Maybe he was a neat freak. Maybe he got it detailed before he departed. Maybe he planned to be back.

Maybe, maybe, maybe.

Pausing on a boardwalk bench, I gazed at the infinity of the Gulf, waves crashing before me, and I beat myself up with the ridiculousness of this whole charade: coming down here to the border of Mexico, wasting money I didn't have, wondering how much time was left before I was evicted from my box of an antiseptic New York City apartment, castigating myself for having the audacity to think I could magically produce a rabbit out of the proverbial hat. It was sheer folly to think that the death of Maggie's father had anything to do with her own plight in prison.

Two tragedies, unconnected.

Even sillier: Me. To let myself get carried away. By what? A photo? By her eternal optimism? Maggie had already released me from any semblance of obligation. She'd said it was all right. She understood there was nothing that could be done about her case. So, what was I doing here? Part of me wanted to return to the ice cream shop and buy a vanilla ice cream. Comfort food. But then I remembered the chirpy clerk. Couldn't stomach that. Blamed it on the meds. I'd been popping so many of them, it was distorting my perspective, allowing me to be overly placid, if not a bit loopy. Toss in the deluge of drink, and, sure, anything would make sense, even the sublime stupidity of my quixotic journey to South Padre Island, surely the end of the earth.

"Mind if I join you?"

Not waiting for an answer was the person asking the question, an elderly gentleman in a wide-brimmed Panama hat. With the aid of a burnished wooden cane, he was already limping precariously toward a seat next to me on the bench when I took note of him.

"Don't have anything better to do," he remarked as he let out a satisfied billow of a sigh on his successful landing, albeit a bit in my personal space. He shook his left leg stiffly.

"Bad knee," he said. "I should warn you. I'm retired, which

means I have a lot of time on my hands to chat about absolutely nothing."

The bench was a bit cramped for my taste but I let it go.

"Be my guest," I said, thinking, here was a genuine candidate. Taking a good look, I could see he was old enough to have been around when the truck was discovered at the pier. I couldn't help noticing he tried to drape his gray hair over a rather large old scar above his left eyebrow. Looked like whatever had caused the scar had been painful. Violent in nature, perhaps. Occupational habit of mine; notice the details. I waited for his opening salvo.

The elderly gentleman gazed out at the ocean. "Nice day," he noted.

There was that word again: *Nice.*

"You could say that," I offered.

"You're not from around here, are you?" he asked without glancing at me.

"How can you tell?"

"Well," he said, "for one, it's the dead of summer, and you look like you haven't seen the sun in a while."

"Got me there," I said.

"And you're not a tourist either," he said, still staring at the Gulf.

"That obvious?"

"It's off-season," he said, "and you're dressed all wrong. You're not wearing a loud Hawaiian shirt or khaki shorts with a fanny pack, and you sure don't look like one of those Spring-breakers."

He should have been the one doing the investigating, not me, I thought.

"Spring-breakers?"

"You know, those college kids who invade the island every March," he said. "Ruins the peace."

"I can imagine," I said. Just keep the conversation going; that's what I reminded myself.

"So, if you don't mind my asking, what brings you to these parts?" he asked, still not looking at me.

There was the opening—organic, not guided. "Actually," I said, "I'm trying to find out about a guy who left a truck down here about thirty years ago and died in an accident in another vehicle not far from Corpus Christi."

At that, the elderly gentleman turned slowly toward me and uttered nothing, but his face gave away that he was thinking. I could almost sense the cogs and wheels grinding on the inside.

What he said was, "Don't know anything about that." But what he didn't say, I could see in the expression of his weary eyes before it hid itself. Something registered. He knew *something*. Not to mention, his profession of ignorance about the truck arrived almost too quickly. He told me he didn't know anything about it before asking more about it. He didn't know enough, based on my brief statement, to say he didn't know anything. If he didn't know anything, he would've first asked more questions about it, to be sure he understood what I was asking him about, but he didn't do that. He recognized something tangible. Instead of addressing it, he rose as quickly as his cane would allow him.

"Must be getting along," he said.

Suddenly, the retiree didn't have all the time in the world anymore.

No exchange of pleasantries. I knew enough not to push it.

What he had said was all I was going to get. It was a hint, a suggestion. It wasn't such a nice day after all. Cane in hand, he hobbled off. Maybe, I mused, remaining planted on the boardwalk bench, my trip to South Padre Island wasn't a complete waste. The mere glimmer of recognition from the elderly gentleman might have been enough of a confirmation, a slight opening.

Sometimes the things not said nor known are the things that count, that tell you something is below the surface.

# 17

After an indulgent evening alone imbibing a bottle of I-can't-remember-alcohol and swallowing a stack of who-knows-pills, I awoke as had become the custom of late, well before sunrise, without the benefit of an alarm blare, stirred to full consciousness by a persistent unease.

As much as I sought to tamp down the embers of my recently concluded destruction, as hard as I distracted myself with the inanity of mindless perambulations, it wouldn't let go of me—the anguish, the haunting, the dread. It was always there, on the cusp.

But this moment—here, now—felt slightly different, off-kilter. It wasn't just the dehydrated hangover, the parched mouth, the pounding headache. There's no accounting for the paranormal, the refracted knowledge of something out of view but felt. Because I knew something was there before I saw it. I sensed it from the moment I opened my eyes, turned over, and lurched from the creaky motel bed on South Padre Island. Even in the dim light peeking through the slats of the ragged, slightly bent window blinds, I could see a piece of paper had been slipped under the door to my room. Shuffling over, I picked it up. Maybe it was a preprinted bill already charged to my card. Maybe not. A note in typed lettering:

DON'T COME BACK.

That's all it said. Effective in its pithiness. The threat was implied. Nothing more needed to be said. In fact, what wasn't said spoke volumes. I sensed the blood pumping faster, my ventricles awakening. I was alert, operating at beyond the normal ten percent capacity of my soporific brain.

I had touched a nerve. I didn't know what it was, but I knew this much: Someone had followed me. I didn't imagine it was the elderly gentleman with the wooden cane whom I'd come across at the boardwalk bench by the Gulf. He hadn't given off the stench of menace. But maybe someone he knew, an associate. I was getting closer to it, whatever *it* was. And they—whoever they were—didn't like it. There was something beyond the stated facts of the death of Maggie's father in that car crash all those years ago. Maybe it was connected to Maggie's case. Or maybe not. And not just that.

Vague utterances came to mind, though not articulated

aloud, and at that moment, it occurred to me I hadn't heard the disembodied voice in some time. It had left me alone, having activated me some time ago, at my lowest ebb, squatting in a pile of New York garbage, setting me off on this careening course to Skiatook and, now, here, to the Mexican border. I guess I was on my own. I could take heed of my own voice anyway. I didn't need the commands of a whispered word.

# 18

Dear Joe,

I'm sorry it's been so long since I've written back. I have to blame it on the bee.

Let me explain. This was back several weeks ago. I was in the day room with a bunch of other trustees. That's what they call us—level 4s—the ones who don't cause any trouble. We keep our heads down.

Well, until now. On this particular day, there was a problem. Somehow or another, a bee got caught inside the day room. It was buzzing around, causing all kinds of havoc. People started squealing and hollering, trying to shoo it away. But there was no way out for the bee. It was bumping up against the windows with no place to go, flailing around. The windows were permanently sealed shut. The door to the day room was locked. It's the way things are around here.

It got to the point where someone tried to smash the bee with her bare hand—but no luck. Someone else was about to swat the bee with a big old book. But missed. Before you knew it, people got all worked up, chanting, "Kill the bee! Kill the bee!"

It got so loud in there. Everyone was screaming. They wanted blood. I don't know what got into me but at that point, I just lost it. The truth is, I wasn't thinking straight when I grabbed the chair. I sure didn't know what I was doing when I flung the chair straight into a window with all of my might. I didn't imagine the glass would shatter the way it did, spraying everywhere. Little shards of glass flew in my face. I'd never done anything like this before. It wasn't me. This isn't how I am.

All I knew was I needed to set that bee free, no matter what. All I knew was that bee just wanted to live.

The next thing I knew, I was being grabbed, shackled, and shoved into the hole. That's what we call isolation around here. You might know it as solitary confinement. It's a small square box of a cell. You can almost touch the walls if you're standing in the middle and reaching out with your hands. There's no human contact. There's nothing in there but you and your thoughts to keep you company.

It's not all bad. The time allowed me to get on my knees and pray to God. But it gets to you after a while, the lack of noise, the lack of light, the lack of everything. You start to feel like the little space is closing in on you. You sit there and talk to yourself. You imagine things. You see things. I was sure I saw that big ball of twine in Kansas. I was convinced I was sitting in that RV, the window open and the wind rushing through my hair. You might've been there. It might've been the only thing that kept me from losing my mind—being in the RV, I mean.

Anyway, when I was released from the hole, I got written up with a misconduct for throwing that chair in the day room. No surprise there. But I figured I should explain to you why you hadn't heard from me in some time. Let's just say I was inconveniently detained by unpleasantries.

Enough about me. I got your last letter, and I'm so sorry to hear about your sorrows. I'm so sorry to hear about what happened to you at the *Herald*. I have no doubt you were right, about what you discovered and what you wrote. You know what you're doing when it comes to investigating wrongful convictions. I have faith in you, Joe. Please don't worry. Things will be set straight.

And thanks for the update about South Padre Island. I can't believe you went all the way down there! What's it like? I've always wondered. I've always pictured people packed at the beach having the time of their lives, sipping pina coladas with those little umbrellas in their drinks. Somehow, I can't imagine you that way, taking it easy, not with the way Mama described you (intense), even though you got rid of your big old beard (thanks for letting me know). Mama would approve, by the way.

What got into you, anyway? Not about the beard. I mean about venturing down to South Padre Island. I'm thankful but I don't have any expectations. I know my case is old, and my father's death doesn't have anything to do with what happened with my case anyway.

I don't know what to make of what you found down there either. Please be careful, Joe. If you were followed and threatened thirty years after my father's death, there's no accounting for what might happen to you next. I don't have a good feeling about this. Please let it be. I guess what I'm saying is, if you don't mind my saying, I'm a bit worried about you.

Blessings,

Maggie

P.S. I still wonder if that bee ever made it out of the day room.

P.S. P.S. Did you get yourself a dog yet?

# 19

It's true, in my last letter to Maggie, I did mention I had shaved my beard. But I failed to note there was another nettlesome problem I couldn't quite rid myself of. A professional problem, as it were. Here it is: I have trouble giving up. I don't know when to let go. Actually, it comes with the territory. An investigative reporter must possess the kind of constitution that blithely forges ahead in the face of persistent failure. You've got to keep running in place against all reason, the oblivious hamster scurrying on the wheel to nowhere, refusing to acknowledge you ought to give up, knowing you're not making any progress, you might never get anywhere, in glorious magnanimous equilibrium. Which I suppose is a form of lunacy.

It was a personal problem, too. If I had had the decency to

know when to quit, I wouldn't still be here. I would've taken care of things by now. I'd be long gone. A distant memory. Maybe not even that. But oh no. I had to go ahead. I had to keep pushing forward.

That's why I had returned to my forlorn laptop on my flimsy card table in my bleak box of an apartment in New York, and did what I'd already done: I looked up Ram.

There was no reason to do this again. I'd done it multiple times before, futilely searching the whereabouts of Maggie's ex, the father of their child, Mary. He'd left a trail of tears—slapped with possession of a controlled dangerous substance, a brief stint in prison, a personal bankruptcy wrought by the purchase of a diamond engagement ring for who knows, a Lasik eye procedure, and a souped-up BMW, a disputed case of arson at an apartment complex where he allegedly lived a while ago. Once, Ram foamed at the mouth when he was pulled over and resisted arrest.

But I'd hit a dead end. He wasn't to be found. He'd fallen off the face of Skiatook, not to be seen in the past three years. I'd already checked the local courts online. There was no reason to go back to my laptop. But for some reason I couldn't account for it, I checked it again, and there was the name of Maggie's ex, blinking on the screen, suddenly reappearing.

Ram had been charged with an unspecified misdemeanor. Had no idea what it was about. The computer didn't offer an answer. Just sparse data. But this much was noted: He was due to show up in a remote courthouse in Skiatook. Now, whether he'd show up was another matter entirely. As a violent offender, ex-con, and habitual felon with a long rap sheet, he might not feel compelled to show up in court to mumble answers in public for a measly misdemeanor. Surely, this was, from his hardened perspective, small potatoes.

But as a hardened investigative reporter, I knew if Ram didn't show up for his court appearance, he'd be courting more trouble, namely, a warrant for his arrest. Sheriff's deputies, with access to more nonpublic information than I had at my fingertips, would likely track him down and haul him before a local magistrate. All of which was saying that he'd likely know what was best for him.

Ram might come to his senses and show up at this courthouse.

Had I told Maggie of my discovery, which I didn't, she might've told me to leave it be. Or she would've told me this wasn't sheer luck, that I stumbled upon Ram. She'd say this was divine intervention, guiding me in the direction of righteousness.

But let's not get carried away. That Ram resurfaced online was due to what I'd attribute to Occam's razor, the simplest explanation. The dude couldn't stay out of trouble. He was bound to pop up, a phenomenon I'd compare to an arcade game of Whac-A-Mole.

That's why I was back in Skiatook, at the wheel of another rental, baking quietly in a deserted parking lot, wondering how many months of credit card debt I could ignore, wondering if Ram would make a cameo appearance for his appointed court hearing.

Rolling around my head was another issue of minor significance. I didn't know what Ram looked like. I figured I'd know him when I saw him. I had an inkling. In one of Maggie's letters, she had mentioned some identifiers. Aside from his Native American heritage, Ram was an MMA fighter. Mixed martial arts. Not a professional fighter. He did it for fun, pummeling others, as an avocation. Not sure that's how he got the nick-name, Ram. But it worked well enough. He liked to ram people, bulldoze them. I pictured he'd be fit and slightly menacing. Not my type. But just my luck. Reason might not work. Words probably wouldn't persuade. This might not end well. Pain might be involved. Maybe he'd do to me what I couldn't quite bring myself to do.

I wasn't sure which would be worse: If he didn't show up, wasting my expensive trip from New York to Oklahoma, or if he did show up and, with alacrity, demonstrated his king of the cage moves on me.

One other issue: I didn't quite know what I'd ask him if he did turn up. I mean, he couldn't possibly know anything about the death of Maggie's father. Ram would've been—what?—an infant then.

And what would Ram say of Maggie's case?

Having reviewed the voluminous trial transcripts—several hundred pages—I knew what he had testified to. That he was asleep on the recliner when Maggie got home from her job as a bartender at the Sooner Second. That he said he awoke to the cry of their child and saw Maggie was tending to Mary in the crib. He corroborated Maggie's account that she was panicked. That she said something was wrong with Mary. That she was going to take the infant to the ER. Strangely enough, Ram even admitted in open court, under oath, what Maggie had told me he said in the heat of the moment that night: "What if we get accused of child abuse?"

Even now, it seemed like a startling question, if not admission.

Why would he worry about such an accusation unless there

was a foundation for it? Was it the first concern when your child is in the midst of a medical emergency? And why didn't the authorities make anything of his statement at the time?

No time to contemplate answers. Not now. There Ram was, striding into my life: compact, coiled, wiry. Almost emaciated. Drug addict? That had to be him. I felt a shot of adrenaline course through me. He'd shown up, after all.

I could take him.

Maybe.

Emerging from what looked like a brand-new red Mustang—how'd he afford that?—Ram strode across the parking lot toward the courthouse with an athlete's ease, though with a slight trace of a limp.

I couldn't read him. Darkened sunglasses obscured his expression. Adding to his near anonymity was a red ball cap, pressed low over his brow, fronted with the caricature of what looked like a Native American warrior in profile with feathers tapering from his black hair. First impression: This was the erstwhile mascot for the old Washington Redskins. Hard to imagine him as a fan. But then it struck me. The hat had nothing to do with the football team. Ram was proudly announcing his Native American heritage.

That was at least one thing to like about him. Otherwise, I'd have to wing it.

"Hey," I called out.

Ram didn't slow his hobbled trot.

"Ram," I said, trying to cut him off at the pass.

Alert to hearing his name being called out, he pulled up his droopy hole-riddled cargo pants, which were at least three sizes too big for him. I had no idea how his pants resisted the force of gravity, not falling in a puddle by his ankles.

"If you come any closer," he said matter-of-factly, "I'll spit in your face."

Not entirely neighborly. Not quite expected either. I didn't particularly want his saliva spewed on my face. In a momentary respite, while I reflected on this unsavory prospect, Ram resumed his hitched gait, swung open the courthouse door, and disappeared within, followed by a woosh of air conditioning. I didn't follow. Instead, I returned to my rental, retrieved a scrap of paper and pen from the glove compartment, and proceeded to jot a note:

RAM, THIS IS ABOUT MAGGIE.
SHE NEEDS YOUR HELP.

And waited.

When Ram finally emerged from the courthouse, into the sweltering heat, I stepped toward him in the parking lot with the note held out, folded. He didn't wait to hear my prologue. With a swiftness that caught me by surprise, he threw an elbow at my jaw, knocking me to the pavement, where he pounced on top of me.

"What do you want?" he seethed.

"It's about Maggie," I said, feeling a miasma of blood seep in my mouth. A sandy ache began to afflict the lower half of my face.

Easing up, he let go of me. I wasn't who he expected. I wasn't a parole officer. I wasn't a repo man. I had no authority over him.

"What about her?" he asked. "She's still in the can, right?"

I didn't lift myself quite yet. I couldn't feel my jaw. "She's still in prison, with another decade to go, but she needs your help."

At this, Ram chuckled derisively and backed off, sitting crossed-legged on the cement, as if pondering the shades of the past.

"Maggie," he said more to himself.

Woozy, I sat up, holding myself in place with my arms extended behind me, like structural support beams.

"Can I be frank with you since we're friends now?" I asked, massaging my jaw.

Ram glanced at me, his head cocked, as if wondering whether he should slam me again for my insolence. Friends? Hardly. Hadn't even given him my name. Acquaintances, more like it. Sometimes, though, I say you just have to meet an MMA fighter where he feels a prickle of a challenge.

"Go ahead," he said, standing up.

I joined him, rising to my feet; there was only so much time I could have remained squatting on the ground of a courthouse parking lot before drawing unwanted attention from people in a position of authority.

"What if," I said, "*you* shook the baby."

"What'd you say?" he snapped.

"Just hear me out," I said tentatively. "Maybe it was a long night. Maybe you were getting a little frustrated. Maybe you were tired. Maybe Mary wasn't feeling well. Maybe she was inconsolable. Maybe she wouldn't sleep. Maybe she kept crying and you didn't know what to do because Maggie was still at work; she'd been out for hours pouring Jack and tap at the

Sooner Second, and you were alone with the baby. So maybe you shook Mary a little harder than you meant to."

Ram stared at me but refrained from responding. I figured another violent elbow might be coming my way. I might duck this time.

"Do you have a death wish?" he asked, though it was more rhetorical.

"Maybe." I didn't want to say yes and scare him away.

"Who are you, anyway?" He was still processing my what-if scenario.

"Nobody," I said. "Just a friend of Maggie's."

"And *this* is what you came here to say?" There was a slither of outrage in his voice.

"Not quite," I said. "What I came here to say is, maybe, just maybe, you didn't mean it. Maybe it just happened. Maybe Maggie had nothing to do with it. Maybe, by the time Maggie got home, it had already happened. The damage had been done. Maybe it was just an accident."

The pause that followed filled the empty parking lot, the waft of a theory: that no one was to blame, technically speaking. That it was no one's fault. Another approach from the investigative reporter's playbook. Offer a scenario to the accused that doesn't quite threaten but brings them a step closer to the truth. If they're willing to admit it might've been an accident, it's a concession on the way to a possible confession.

"What if it was?" Ram said, folding his arms.

"What if *what* was?" I asked back.

"What if it was an accident?"

It was a question but it felt like more. Was Ram admitting to something more, an accident gone bad, an accident that wasn't an accident? This might be as close as he ever gets to admitting culpability. From the rolodex of previous investigations: With some of the most heinous crimes imaginable, involving not just sociopaths but psychopaths, where remorse is an abstraction, there's often an urgent need to tell someone. To admit what they did—even to a stranger. In my book, Ram was shaping up to pre-qualify as at least a sociopath. It wasn't just his reflexive need to spit in my face. The violent elbow placed him squarely in the province of other sociopaths I'd come across. Attack first, the credo went, ask questions later.

"Well, then it was an accident," I said as if that settled it.

"I'm not saying it was," Ram was quick to note. "Nobody got convicted of child abuse, mind you. Maggie just got nicked for neglect."

"I know," I was equally quick to say, trying to loosen the valve. "Look, it was a decade ago."

"A long time ago," he concurred.

"Water under the bridge," I said, instantly lashing myself for trotting out the cliché. Couldn't escape the writer that was me.

And why was I being so agreeable with him?

"Can barely remember what happened," he said. "Sometimes, I wonder if what I remember actually happened. Feels like a dream—a bad dream."

"I know the feeling," I said, and I did.

Ram peered at me, and even through his sunglasses, I sensed a softening.

"I bet you do," he said, inspecting me. "Listen, I gotta go."

But he didn't move. I guess I couldn't camouflage the flotilla of wreckage that was me, especially from someone else who was marooned in his own wreck, though in a different way.

"I don't suppose . . ." I faltered, not sure how to phrase what I was about to emit. I didn't need to. He knew where I was going.

"Can't help you, Bud," he said.

"Maggie's got ten more years to go," I said. "Don't know how she's going to make it."

The sympathy card. Maybe he'd feel bad for her, or not. He was turning away from me. Too much to expect from an ex. Not to mention, Maggie seemed to be managing just fine. Small detail. Overlooked. She was faring better than I was, in fact. Even with the bee incident. No accounting for madness, hers or mine. There was no time for niceties, so I called out to Ram, "Would you be willing to admit it was an accident?"

He turned back. He slumped his shoulders, casting himself in a withered, concave look. There was no MMA fight in him. Maybe he had a conscience.

"I ain't going back to the can," he said. "No matter what."

I nodded my head. "Right," I said. "I get it."

Over the years, I'd heard variations on the same theme during my investigations, echoes of detachment from other people that drove home my cynicism about humanity. They'd say: Can't help you. I have a family to feed. I'd be killed if I told you anything. I don't want to get involved. Get off my lawn.

"By the way," he asked offhand, "how's Mary since the—ah—incident?"

Right. Mary. Why hadn't I thought of her? Ram hadn't seen his little girl—Maggie's little girl—since the incident. Another curated word. *Incident.* A decade of absence. A lifetime. He'd just walked out, away. Ram probably didn't even know Mary had survived, thrived.

"Beautiful child," I said, parroting what Maggie's mama had told me.

"That right?" His voice squeaked higher than average.

"Healthy as an ox," I added. No need to mention I was merely conveying what I'd heard secondhand. Why are ox so healthy, while we're at it? Needed to get back to reading literature. My pickled mind was overrun with tired phraseology, benumbed by pills, waterlogged with cheap liquor.

"One other thing," Ram asked. "What was in the note?"

"What note?" I was still pondering my penchant to produce aphorisms.

"The note," he said, "the one you were going to give me."

I'd already forgotten what I'd scribbled a moment ago. The scrap of paper was lying on the ground, crumpled. Needed editing.

"Oh, that," I said. "Nothing."

He nodded. Accepted not knowing. He'd done a lot of that, I figured.

"What were you here for?" I asked, gesturing at the courthouse behind us.

"Huh?"

"What was the charge?"

"Shoplifting," he said, taking off his sunglasses. There was a deep well of preexisting pain in his dark eyes.

"I'm sorry," he said quietly.

About the shoplifting? About Maggie? About Mary? About what he might've done? About what he almost admitted to? About what he couldn't quite confess?

"About what?"

"About the elbow to your face," he said. "No offense."

Without meaning to, I almost found myself liking Ram. For all of his violence and pimped-out bravado, he couldn't quite mask his own troubled contemplation. I could see he'd been living with a heavy burden for a time. Maybe longer than I had. There was anguish everywhere. I nodded and said, "None taken."

# 20

Tally was locked in executive mode, ready to slay suits, moments before heading off to her corner office located among the masters of the universe in midtown Manhattan. But before she departed, my sister halted at the front door and turned back to me.

"Tell Maggie the truth," she said.

I was still half asleep on the plush cushions of her tailored living room couch.

"What truth?" I asked.

"That Ram did it," she said.

"He didn't admit to the crime," I said, sitting up.

"He all but did," Tally said.

In my sister's world, she had a way of simplifying what was before her, distilling things to their essence.

"Ram posed it as a conditional," I said. "'What if it was an accident?' That's far from admitting that he hurt his own child. Besides, what he said isn't admissible. He'd have to swear to it in an affidavit."

"So?" Tally was looking at me impatiently.

"So?"

"So, get him to do that," she ordered.

"Might be a bit tricky," I said, "especially when he made it clear he's not willing to implicate himself and go back to prison."

Tally nodded her head. More clarity. She didn't have time to waste on futile endeavors. "But the real question is: Did he do it?"

"Sure looks like it," I said.

"Or maybe he didn't," she said, arching a brow.

We nodded at each other. A simple accord between siblings. An implicit understanding without words. That was the end of that.

If I was willing to admit the truth, it was that Tally was usually right. She was my secret weapon in virtually every investigation I'd conducted. She was the one who could spot the hidden trend. She was the one who would identify the culprit when I was looking elsewhere. She'd find the evidence that unlocked the case. Tally should've been on the payroll, if I had one.

Her brain always operated at a higher plane than mine, going back to our broken childhood. She'd say what I was thinking before I completed the thought. To wit: An adult would ask me a question. I would begin to open my mouth. But before the words emerged, Tally would intervene and speak on my behalf. My spokesperson. I would close my mouth. Tally was my conscience, my memory, my reality check. She was the talent in the family. I was the mule. I carried the heavy objects. A beast of burden.

"What are you going to do now?" she asked.

"No idea," I said morosely.

"Maybe it's time to let it go," she said.

"Can't," I said faster than I meant to.

"Why not?"

Good question. Why not? What was wrong with me? Why couldn't I let it go? I hadn't asked myself the obvious question. It had resided beneath the surface, wallowing just out of reach of consciousness, nagging at the edge of my hypothalamus.

But I did know. Hesitating, I stole a look at Tally, wondering if she could read the worry afflicting me as she always could. There were no secrets between us, not after everything.

"I heard a voice," I said tightly.

"What voice?"

"A voice, you know."

Now I wasn't peering at Tally. I knew she was gawking at me.

"Whose voice?" she persisted. There was a deliberateness in her tenor.

"Don't know. Just some voice."

"A voice attached to a person?" Tally asked clinically.

"No."

"Oh, great," she said, letting out a beleaguered sigh. "You mean, like a *voice*."

"Right."

"What did the voice say?"

"Listen, I don't want to talk about it," I said.

It had actually been a while since I'd heard the voice. What's more, it hadn't said much when it had spoken. In fact, there was enough room for interpretation in what the voice whispered to conclude that it had nothing to do with Maggie or investigating her old case. *Look. Go.* Those invocations could apply to anything.

Then again, to my way of thinking, it was better to blame my foolish excursions into Maggie's case on a disembodied voice than my own unprompted idiocy.

"Joe," Tally said, elongating the vowels with disappointment.

"Don't say it," I said, though I didn't know what she was about to say. I just knew I wouldn't like it.

"You can't save *every* mother," she said.

"What're you talking about?"

"You know what I'm talking about," she said, holding her ground.

"This has nothing to do with Mom," I said defensively, realizing it sounded like I doth protest too much.

"Are you sure?"

"Yes." (No, I wasn't sure.)

Tally was treading precariously close to what we never revisited, a shared personal past with a family history we had sealed shut long ago out of respect for the memory of our mother, not to mention Tally's own narrative born of inexplicable loss. For her, being a single mother was enough without dissecting the undergirding.

Overcome with a sudden deluge of fatigue, I rose from the couch. Lightheaded, I needed to get out of there. But Tally beat me to it. She had to get to work. She turned at the front door and didn't bother to say goodbye on her way out. I knew what Tally was thinking. She was thinking I had finally cracked. Lost my mind. Maybe I had.

# 21

That night, I couldn't turn off the spigot of relentless thoughts, no matter how hard I tried to divert myself with the benign and the meaningless. For a time, I imagined I was shipwrecked on a tropical island with a motley crew of misfits, including one barefoot beauty. We'd build little huts, a long rectangular table for feasts of coconut milk and fresh fish. We'd entertain ourselves by erecting a quaint amphitheater where I'd write comedies performed by the stranded. No luck. Still wide awake. Elbowing into the narrative: whiffs of destruction and despair.

The ruination of the recent past peeked around the corner of my mind. The disaster of the story that took me down. The massive correction, published on Page One, followed by the disgrace, the departure, the deluge of ceaseless vitriol on social media.

Swift, permanent.

I couldn't help but retrace my steps and second-guess myself, wondering where I might've gone wrong in that last *Herald* investigation, my personal waterloo. I had corroborated every detail of every published word under my byline. I had multiple sources. I'd triangulated the three-part series with public and confidential documents.

What had I missed?

Behind that recent and public calamity reared the past beyond the past—the monstrous head of an earlier private anguish—that which Tally and I never dared broach aloud as siblings in confidence. Our mother. Mom. A death without reasonable explanation. The unanswered questions. I couldn't quite remember the details. It eluded my flooded memory banks, just so. I was too young when it happened. All that I knew for sure was our father maintained his innocence and continues to do so. We left it alone. Some things are just too painful to confront.

At least I admitted the obvious. What happened back then accounted for how I got into this crazy racket. I wasn't an investigative reporter for nothing. I didn't probe wrongful convictions for no reason. This line of work didn't come from nowhere. It made sense in the bright logic of sad circumstance. I was merely a byproduct of my tumultuous environment. Or so I thought as I readjusted my sleeping position fitfully. I couldn't get comfortable. I couldn't coax myself to sleep. I could only feel a thin layer of perspiration coating my forehead. That, and a deep pit of dread in the center of my stomach. I couldn't quite believe this was my life. If I had known this was where it was going to land, I wouldn't have waited around for it. I recalled my official second-grade classroom photo: me, gap-toothed with too much hair, a la the Beatles' shag, staring amiably into an unseen camera, unaware of the terrible things to come. *Why hadn't Mom gotten me a decent haircut before picture day?* Part of me wondered if I had simply imagined it all, not just the ruination but the rest of it too. Maybe there was no Maggie. Could she have been a product of my creative faculties? Perhaps I didn't inhabit the sterile box of an apartment that confined me in this moment, as I wrestled with the dying light, unable to find rest, sleep, or peace. It was as if my brain was overheating, taxing the operating system, straining the gears and wiring, ratcheting up the levels of distress toward DEFCON 1—nuclear.

The more I tried to will myself to sleep, the more alert I became. The more I sought to use brute force to anesthetize myself with florid images of nothingness, the more I saw the stark horrors of my existence. I didn't want to be me. No. That wasn't it. I hated that I was me. It was like I was Krazy-glued to this person I couldn't stand, stuck in a quicksand of utter disgrace, a smothering of disappointment.

Bolting up, I thought I was hyperventilating. I couldn't quite make out the dark shapes filling the stillness of night. My pupils hadn't dilated. My retinas hadn't been reached. But something else had been triggered, a subversive thought. In the vacuum of sight, I became aware of my brain's presence, how it had been working something out in the background, without making me aware of the effort. It had an idea; not about me, but about Maggie's case. Why hadn't I thought of *this* before? Daylight was still hours away but I'd reached a resolution; it was time to rise.

# 22

On my way back to Skiatook, I drove past the now-familiar grain silos, whipped by the old water tower, and took nary a glance at the stripped-down truck propped up on cinderblocks. I made a pit stop at the Sooner Second, where I earned a sniff of vague recognition from the expressionless barkeep. Go figure. At the rate of my reappearances, throwing back a shot of Jack, I was threatening to become a regular, if not a local. I wasn't, by the way, downing a shot of Jack to wash myself away. I was taking a shot of liquid courage.

That's what was required in my approach to Enos. He'd already slammed a door in my face weeks back. He'd already told me to leave him alone. He'd already warned me more death could follow if I didn't leave alone the unanswered questions about the fatal car crash that he'd survived, that decades ago had claimed the life of his best friend, Maggie's father.

But an eternal principle of investigative journalism had clutched at me in the middle of the night, grasping at my sense of commitment, my resolution, rousing me from my unquenchable misery; that is, you can't take no for an answer when you're digging for the truth, not if you're an investigative reporter. I mean, of course, you do take no for an answer, but not before you've confirmed a no is a no, not a maybe, or a let me think about it because I wish I could say something, if I could only bring myself to do the right thing.

There is, for the investigative reporter, an inexhaustible optimism perceived in unvarnished defeat. Yes, Enos had refused to speak with me the last time I came knocking on his door at his shack down by the junkyard in Skiatook. But there was this: Words had passed. He'd articulated what he didn't want to do, which was to speak to me. Not terribly helpful. But in the *not* speaking to me, he had actually spoken to me. He didn't have to do that. He could have spared himself the act of opening the door to ward me off. To put a positive spin on it, the door was slightly ajar—figuratively and literally. And that's all I needed to pry it further open, to get him to tell me more. Which was why I was returning to confront him.

Granted, it wasn't much to go on. Perhaps even a bit of a stretch to purchase another plane ticket from New York's LaGuardia. But that's how these things tended to play out, the investigation hanging on by a thread of the fantasy of a breakthrough.

"Enos?"

The shock of white hair accosted me before his arch of

surprise at the sight of me in the shimmering heat. He recognized me without the biblical beard.

"You again," he said, the words dripping with disdain as he opened his front door a smidge. "I thought I told you to leave me alone."

"Just have one question," I said, though that wasn't exactly true.

My impromptu utterance took an iota of a second to convey. Less than three seconds to go before he slams the door in my face. One question, one second. Not much of a commitment. Actually, what I'd said wasn't entirely false. It was more of an *untruth*. In a different category than a lie. Inhabiting another rubric. I mean, I could ask just one question, even if I harbored others.

Couldn't I?

I was almost instantly exhausted from my own mental contortions.

"You're gonna git' me killed," Enos said, scanning the Beirut-like terrain behind me: a vast expanse of dry dirt and corrugated metal scraps intermingling with scats of garbage fluttering in the hot wind of summer desolation. This was the view from Enos' front yard, a dystopian lunar-like universe.

How could my presence get Enos killed? Who was he searching for behind me? Did it have to do with the death of Maggie's father?

I'd have to reserve those questions for another time. When there was time. *If* there was time.

"Then let me inside," I said. "I've come all the way from New York."

Translation: My request to speak with Enos must be important. Also, costly. The synapses fired without enough time for me to think through the suggestion. That's what happens when I'm desperate. Let the unconscious take over. Hope it knows what it's doing.

Talk about faith.

"Make it quick," Enos said, opening the door just wide enough for me to pass through and follow his shadow into the darkness within.

So, it worked. At least for the next, oh, say, three minutes. Before he kicked me out for good. He left the front door ajar. Message conveyed: I wasn't to stay long. He didn't want to expend all that kinetic energy closing a door because he knew he'd have to open it a moment later to remove *moi* from his premises, possibly forcibly.

Enos didn't even bother to sit down to establish the formalities of a conversation. Standing in a cramped, dingy room that served as a living room, dining room, and office all at once, he turned back toward me. There wasn't much room for me to maneuver. We stood there facing each other, invading each other's personal space. He stank of gin. I gave off a whiff of Jack.

Pick your poison.

"I know you're lying," I said.

Not sure why I picked that opening. The frontal approach. Lacked nuance. But my id was in charge at the moment, and my superego was allowing it to navigate the channels of this burgeoning fiasco.

"Don't have the foggiest idea whatcha talkin' about," Enos said.

Almost expected him to spit derisively on the dirty hardwood floor. To remove the distaste from his mouth. He didn't.

Civilized beast, that one.

"Not that I blame you," I said. Better. Dialed back. More polite. Less invasive.

"Still don't know what you're talkin' about, mister," he said.

I'd just been upgraded to a mister, a position of authority. Why the respect? Time for poker. Not one of my strong suits. But I'd have to play this card. Didn't have another at my disposal.

"There's more to the story," I stated as fact.

(Was there? ((No idea.)))

My eyes must've adjusted to the dimness surrounding us. I caught wind of Enos doing a double take before recovering, containing himself.

"What story?" he squawked.

"There's more to the story about the death of Maggie's father," I said, still bluffing.

"What difference is it to you?"

Well now.

That was what we folks in the trade called a nondenial denial.

Enos didn't deny there was more to the story of the death of Maggie's father, the one where Enos was at the wheel of the vehicle when he allegedly dozed off and swerved headlong into an eighteen-wheeler, killing Maggie's father, who was supposedly riding shotgun. Enos just recalibrated his response with a question.

Perhaps we were getting somewhere.

"Makes no difference to me," I said. (It did.) "But makes a big difference to Maggie. She deserves to know the truth about her *father*."

Almost said papa. Too much. Maybe pa was more appropriate. Stuck with father. Universal enough. Wanted to leave

Enos with the emphasis on the familial, punctuate the word, and stick the landing.

He might even empathize.

"The *truth*." Enos chuckled, stuck on that word. But he wasn't laughing. He was chiding the word itself, *truth*, as if it were mocking him, the fool.

"Yes," I pushed forth, "the truth."

"Whatever that means," Enos said dismissively. Now he was the junkyard philosopher, musing on the existential in a dilapidated shack.

I took a different approach, seeking to elicit sympathy. "The truth means something to Maggie," I said, going with a hint of righteous indignation because what else did I have? "After a decade in prison, the truth means a lot to Maggie. When she's got another decade to go, the least Maggie deserves is the truth about what happened to her father."

Three times, I had just cited her name: Maggie. Maggie. Maggie. To personalize the appeal, a prayer for the imprisoned.

Enos was shuffling in place but his voice was dialing down into a lower octave.

"Yeah, well, what d'ya know?" he asked, and I could see he was trying to take the measure of me. "Are ya a God-fearing man?"

A curveball.

What did his question about God have to do with anything? This always happened. Humans were messy, asymmetrical. This is why I avoided them of late. Except now. Maggie's case had drawn me out into daylight, from the cave, so to speak, though it didn't seem like it at the moment. I was, as a matter of fact, standing in a darkened room next to a broken-down old man who had just asked me the ultimate question.

"Listen," I stammered.

I was teetering on the cliff of nothingness, not knowing where I was going with the beginning of that sentiment. Listen. Listen?

To what?

My mind was scampering to complete the sentence, to eject other words that would resemble something coherent, maybe even slightly compelling. But it didn't. The ghost in the machine stalled.

Reverted back to factory settings. I wasn't a God-fearing man. I wasn't only godless. I was speechless. I could think of no reason why I was still standing there. I could think of no reason why Enos should speak to me. I could think of no reason why he shouldn't toss me out on my derriere, excuse my French, to borrow the expression of Maggie's mama. The truth was—speaking of the truth—there was no good reason why Enos should tell me the truth, whatever it was, no matter how inconvenient. Clearly, it was a risk, a hazard to his health, maybe mine, though I could live with that burden. Enos couldn't. He turned away from me, departing our little tete-a-tete, shuffling to his cluttered desk, where he busied himself by burrowing into a towering pile of what, in the shadows, gave off the distinct appearance of trash.

"Ah," he said to himself. "There it is."

I caught the crisp click of a nob of a contraption being turned on. What ensued was a buzz of static, followed by a low thrum of a banjo, the entrails of country music emanating from a transistor radio that more rightly belonged in a museum than a shack.

As tempting as it was, I resisted the urge to ask Enos why

we needed atmospheric radio tunes at this particular moment. As much as I might appreciate the crooning of a love long lost at a gas station or some such—I was never one to catch the precise lyrics—I didn't quite see how country music applied to the circumstances.

"Reckon they're always listening," Enos said as he shuffled back toward me. "The music will drown 'em out."

My brain chugged back to life, spewing out questions to myself: *Who* is listening? *What* are they listening to? And *why* are they being drowned out? I remained mute. The look on my face said nothing, a cipher.

"You know," Enos said, sighing, "I'm tired of holding onto *this*."

It was his way of saying I couldn't take any credit for what he was about to unload, *this*, a thirty-year-old secret. Sometimes, it's just a matter of timing, being in the right place at the right time.

"Can I trust you?" he asked, squinting in the darkness.

"Yes." More accurate: He wanted to trust me.

"How do I know I can trust you?"

Another existential question without a neat answer.

"You know you can trust me," I said, selling sincerity. More precise: He didn't know but he needed to.

"You're right," he said with a harrumph.

This is what happens. The thing is, the concealed is tough to hoard. Especially the kind that haunts you.

"He's alive."

That's all Enos said. Just like that. Uttered with the aplomb of announcing the weather. Hot day. A real humdinger, as they might say in Skiatook.

"What're you saying?" I asked, even though I knew. I just

needed to hear it to make sure I heard right, that I wasn't imagining things.

"Luke," he said, toggling to a whisper. "He's alive."

The name he hadn't articulated in decades. Luke. His old friend. Maggie's father. The one who was supposed to have been asleep, riding shotgun in the car when Enos, strapped in his seatbelt, allegedly dozed off, drifting headlong into an eighteen-wheeler. Luke, who should be dead, was just brought back to life.

"He survived the wreck?" I asked, disbelieving.

"Not exactly," Enos said, before adding, "He wasn't in no wreck."

Stunned, I tried to comprehend the import of his admission. "*What?*"

"We staged it," Enos said, shifting uncomfortably in place. "The whole thing. Lodged a brick by the gas pedal to keep the car in acceleration. Dumped the car in a ditch in the middle of nowhere to make it look like a crash. Paid off a sheriff's deputy to report it as an accidental fatality, DOA. Cost a pretty penny. But we had more than enough cash. Not that we gave the deputy any choice. Take the cash or we set the cartel loose on the poor soul. I came back to Skiatook with an urn full of ashes."

Enos made it sound so simple. DOA. Dead on arrival.

"Whose ashes were they?"

As soon as I asked the question, I berated myself. Did it matter whose ashes they were? Why did I need to know? Wasn't it a secondary—maybe a tertiary—point?

"It was nobody's ashes," Enos said, shrugging. "We set fire to a dead squirrel we found on the side of the road. Added some dirt to the mix."

Not even a human facsimile. A squirrel. Roadkill. That's what I had been searching for when I paid a visit to the cemetery looking for Luke's headstone. Don't know why that irritated me. More relevant: It must've been easier to fake a death back thirty years ago on a deserted road in the middle of Nowhere, Texas.

And where did a yokel like Enos, he of the shack by the junkyard, and his buddy, Luke, come up with more than enough cash to bribe a local member of law enforcement, a sheriff's deputy? This was not an insignificant criminal infraction. Even more to the point, I found myself asking aloud: "Why did Luke fake his death?"

Enos scratched his chin as if he was trying to think of a good reason. Instead, he turned around and raised the volume of country music blaring on the radio. Just in case.

"The cartel," he whispered.

"The what?"

"The *cartel,*" Enos repeated, even softer, for fear of being overheard. "Luke stole *drug* money from the cartel. You don't do that. Not ever. Unless you want to be found murdered real quick."

"Drug money?" I repeated the phrase but gathered the meaning instantly. Just as Maggie had suspected of her father, Luke must've been ferrying illicit stuff—who knows what, marijuana, coke, meth—across the border into the United States. Enos, for his part, must've been in cahoots with Luke. But, judging by the looks of his whereabouts, in the vicinity of an unromantic junkyard, the drug business didn't do much for Enos financially.

But. It didn't take much to make the logical leap: that Luke and Enos had been drug runners, given the location of Luke's abandoned vehicle on the shores of South Padre Island at the intersection of Texas and Mexico. It was widely known the cartels established massive warehouses packed with drugs along the Mexican side of the border for easy distribution northward to where the moneyed customers resided: in the United States. The rest, though, didn't compute.

"Luke stole a *lot* of drug money," Enos said as a point of clarification.

"What's a lot?"

"Enough to get yourself disappeared into the Mexican countryside with a new identity and a new lifestyle," he said with a cluck. "That's for sure."

"Enough to pay off a sheriff's deputy to report him dead," I added.

"Yep," Enos nodded. "The coroner, too."

"The *coroner?*"

"Had to pay him off, too," Enos said. "Ain't no big deal. He wasn't even a medical doctor. Just some guy in a town appointed to the highfalutin position, *coroner.* Makes the death official, a certificate and all."

Given the number of people involved—a sheriff's deputy, a coroner, and at least one old friend, Enos himself—it was remarkable that Luke's fake death had held up for thirty years without collapsing in on itself. But then again, this was orchestrated near a small town, Luke was practically a kid, a nobody from Oklahoma, and there was no accounting for the effectiveness of that most eternal of human motives, the pied piper of greed. The Greeks had it right. There were only so many forms of tragedy.

"Where is Luke now?" I asked.

"Don't know," Enos said tightly.

"You must have some idea."

"Haven't spoken to Luke in thirty years," Enos said. "He made sure I didn't know where he went. In case—" Here, he caught his breath.

"In case of what?"

"In case I was tortured," he said flatly.

Oh, right. Torture. A cartel specialty. I'd read their press clippings.

"Of course," I said just as flatly.

"But," Enos said, raising a finger.

"But?"

"If it were me—"

"—Yes?" I interrupted.

"I'd head somewhere in the middle of Mexico."

"Don't know about that," I quipped. "I'd choose the coast. Ocean view."

"There's that," Enos remarked. "But this ain't no summer vacation. If you want to get lost for good, you'd best be wandering off somewhere smack dab in the middle of the crowds, the smog, the traffic jams. Hidden in plain sight. Just my opinion, mind you."

Enos gave me a look I couldn't quite interpret in the darkness.

Was he offering a hint?

Or was it just a guess?

Or a personal preference?

Too many questions. There was this one, too: "How," I asked, "is Luke's fake death connected to Maggie's case of criminal neglect?"

Enos squinted hard at me: "Don't know what you're talking about."

"What about Luke's truck?" I pursued down another avenue. "Why was it found perfectly scrubbed—immaculate—down by the pier on South Padre Island?"

Enos let loose a small whistle between his yellowed teeth. "Immaculate? Big five-dollar word, that there. Can't tell you, mister. Luke didn't leave it all cleaned up, that's for sure. Man was a slob. Left Cheetos everywhere. Beer bottles, too. Luke didn't have no plans to retrieve his vehicle after faking his death. The cartel must've located his truck once they got wind of the car accident. They coulda been trying to remove any evidence."

"Of what?"

Enos shrugged: "Drugs. Fingerprints. Blood stains. Who knows?"

Blood stains? Whose blood stains? I let it go. Not entirely relevant.

"And why didn't you fake your own death?" I asked.

"That's easy enough," he said. "I didn't steal no money from no cartel."

Enos seemed ready for that question. Maybe he didn't have the taste for money the way Luke did. Or perhaps Enos did but didn't need to display the trappings of wealth. Omitted from our interrogatory was my suspicion of his own role as a drug runner. The timing didn't seem right. He seemed ready to end the conversation as he made for the front door, holding it open for me.

"I've told you plenty," he said. "Consider it a gift to Luke's little girl. I owe Maggie that much. But you're gonna have to figure out the rest on your own."

In the game of poker, you need to know when to fold.

"Your secret is safe with me," I said, adding trade lingo for good measure: "Off the record."

"Yeah, well, I ain't worried about it," Enos snorted. "If you know what's good for you, young man, you'll leave the whole thing alone, or—"

"—Or what?"

"—Or," he said, blankly, "you'll get yourself killed."

Enos cracked a gap-toothed grin. He wasn't smiling, though. It wasn't a threat. He was merely stating a fact. Not sure which one, though. The fact that he would kill me if I spilled the secrets? Or that the cartel would murder me? Did it make any difference?

I grinned back at him. I wasn't smiling either.

# 23

Dear Joe,

I have to admit, I don't know quite what to say about your last letter and what you've discovered. I don't know what is more shocking: Ram all but admitting to the crime that got me put away, or my father being alive when I always thought he was long gone.

Like you, I don't see the connection between the two things. What happened to my father occurred decades before what happened to my Mary. It's almost too much to bear when I try to take it all in. I look around me, and I'm just a bystander to the insanity. Nothing changes. People yell a lot around here. There's minor drama about who's not talking to who. I sleepwalk through the days and nights, and no one has any idea what's happening out there in the real world, what with Ram and his assorted crimes, Enos and his little old shack by the junkyard doing who knows what. And my father, wherever he is, whoever he is.

All I can say is, leave it be, Joe. I don't need to know any more. I never knew my father anyway. You've told me enough. It doesn't change anything. I'm still in here and I can't do anything about it except pray. At least I don't have to wonder what happened to my father anymore. It's buried in the past. The truth is, I'm more worried about the present. I'm concerned about you, Joe. You've dug deep enough. You don't want to dig any deeper. You've been threatened. I don't like that anonymous note left under your motel door. I don't like the warning from Enos. Knowing him like I used to, he meant it when he told you to leave things alone or you'll get yourself killed. So, please, I'd rather focus on the future. I'd rather imagine riding along in that RV, my hair flying, on a road trip to anywhere. Let it go, Joe.

Blessings,

Maggie

P.S. In my dream the other night, I caught a glimpse of the dog of your future. She's a vicious little mutt, a cross between a Mini Pinscher and a Chihuahua. But don't worry, she's pretty cute.

# 24

Maybe, the voice I thought I heard all those weeks ago hadn't uttered a word. Maybe I didn't hear anything. Maybe I just made up the whole thing, a phantasmagorical residue of the cocktail of pills and drink stewing in my wracked unconsciousness.

It had been such a long time since I thought I heard the whispered incantations. *Look. Go.* And there had been no follow up. No other instructions. Nothing. Not a single other word. There was reasonable doubt. Maybe Tally was right. My little sister usually was. Maybe this wasn't about Maggie and her tragic case. Maybe it wasn't about her father, Luke, and his odd disappearance into the Mexican countryside. Maybe it was really about Mom. I couldn't let it go. My mom's passing remained an unresolved riddle of dusty memory, even if the official cause of death left little to interpretation—a single gunshot to the head.

My father always maintained his innocence but to no avail; he sat rotting in prison, awaiting the ultimate punishment: the death penalty. And yet, I could never bring myself to act on my suspicions. That there was more to my father's case. It was the only investigation I couldn't bring myself to confront when given the opportunity. Whenever I allowed myself to think about what happened, I was overcome with enervation. I was seized with a paralysis of inaction. Perhaps, I was afraid of what I would discover, that my father was guilty as charged, and I would have to let go of the last hope.

My own recent ruination added a layer of desensitization. I couldn't address my own destruction; how could I help my father with his?

It didn't matter that what I had written in my last published investigation in the *Herald* was accurate. The story had been repudiated by my bosses. It didn't take much to undermine my findings. Just a single source who, for reasons that eluded me, reversed course, claiming after publication that he didn't tell me what he'd told me, despite my handwritten notes to the contrary.

It was like pulling the pin from a grenade; my source's public disavowal instantly blew up my life, with a correction on Page One, recanting my entire investigation. The reverberations from the blast came in the form of social media, with rants on Twitter castigating me, and vitriol on Facebook calling for my head on a pike. The invective went viral, a hashtag of disgrace. In an instant, I was radioactive, less than nothing, convicted online and condemned to what felt like a civil version of a life sentence, trapped in my own form of imprisonment, built with an invisible perimeter, like a dog confined within a wireless fence—wander too far, and I'd get zapped with a painful electric shock.

There was no escaping, not when I temporarily shook off the shackles of my box of an apartment in the suffocation of New York City. The ruination stayed with me wherever I was, even now, standing in the middle of a bustling market square, unsure what to do next. I was, for lack of a better term, winging it. There was no plan; nothing to go on, except what Enos had alluded to about getting lost in the middle, about going where the crowds went, about hiding in plain sight amid smog and traffic jams. About being in Mexico City.

It had to be here. Where else fit the description, given the circumstances? Luke, Maggie's father, had disappeared into Mexico. That much Enos, Luke's best friend, seemed to insinuate. The rest was without detail, an educated guess, a matter of feel. That's why I booked a flight without giving it a second thought, worried not at all about the mounting credit card debt—the worse it got, the less it seemed to matter—and I landed in the capital city without knowing where I'd stay for the night. An insignificant detail. I hadn't rested peacefully in I couldn't remember when. Even when I slept, I wasn't asleep. My body was agitated. My mind was walking in circles.

This had to be where I'd find Luke. Unless, of course, it wasn't. Unless Enos was just spitballing. Unless Enos had no idea what he was talking about. Unless Luke was nowhere near Mexico City. What Enos had said might've been simply the ramblings of an old buddy with no knowledge about where Luke was—a friend who likely had a new name, a new life. In which case, I was just a fool in a foreign land, staring at a sea of people streaming before me in bright colors, hawkers, and caballeros, speaking in a staccato of Spanish I couldn't comprehend. An old church with an ornate gold dome towered in the background, neglected in the rush of passersby, conspicuously out of place.

What, though, was the alternative? I'd already exhausted all of the databases at my disposal, coming up blank when searching for variations on Luke's identity. He'd not only disappeared. He didn't exist, at least in the digital ether. More problematic was that I didn't know what he looked like now, at least thirty years since he vanished. All I knew was what Maggie had said, that her father was a tall drink of water. An American, he'd be about fifty years old or so now. In my pocket, I still had that frayed old photo of Luke as a young man with the crooked grin. My description of Luke applied to countless hombres down in these parts. The identifiers weren't narrowed down much.

I wasn't even sure what I'd ask him if I found him in the middle of the haystack. To confirm Enos's story? That Luke had stolen boatloads of money from the cartel? To what end? What would I do with that admission? Ask him to help his daughter whom he'd never met? And how? I still couldn't see a remote connection between his disappearance and his daughter's conviction on a criminal neglect charge three decades later. The missing puzzle pieces were too numerous, leaving me groping in the dark to understand which way was up. My disorientation was magnified by a growing dread: What was I doing in Mexico? Why couldn't I leave well enough alone? Couldn't I take a hint? *Don't come back. You'll get yourself killed.* What was wrong with me?

I couldn't firewall my lashing doubts from spreading into a wave of panic. I was untethered, too far removed from any semblance of a tangible lead. There were too many variables, the investigative options were limitless. Maybe, I told myself, this is nothing more than the mad preoccupation of a wild goose chase.

# 25

Urgently needing to escape, I was acutely aware I stood out like an archetype of the bewildered gringo in the wrong part of Mexico with a backpack strapped to my sweaty shoulders. I could feel the heat in the kaleidoscope of stares in the town square. I sensed the opprobrium in the blank eyes that penetrated me. I could see what they saw: a lost soul from foreign environs unknown. Jostled in a throng of strangers, I was stricken with the pang of loneliness. Maybe I was just attempting to run away from myself, preoccupying myself with busyness because of the extreme vacuity of my own existence.

"Hola."

When I turned toward the mellifluous voice, I was greeted by a meretricious lipstick smile, before I took in the rest: a face with impossibly big dolorous dark eyes which were masked by colorful makeup.

"Americano?" she queried.

"Si," I nodded, looking for a quick exit.

"Mi nombre es Vera," she said, pointing a long red fingernail at herself.

"Joe," I said, pointing at my less effusive self.

"Ven conmigo," she said, gesturing to follow her as she strode off in plastic high heels.

I didn't budge. Didn't know what she had said but I had no intentions of going off with Vera. I assumed that was just a stage name, incidentally. She had rolled the "r" in Vera, for whatever that was worth. I had important matters to attend to, anyway. I was tracking down a missing man, Maggie's father Luke. I didn't have time for dalliances—or the inclination. Not that I would even consider it.

"Joe," she called out, waving at me.

So, I followed her.

Didn't even protest. Just started walking behind her. Don't know why. It just happened. My feet reacted before my brain could weigh in on the decision. Was I being polite? No. The compliance was born of something else. I didn't have anywhere to go. I didn't have anything to do. I was profoundly lost. I had no plan. In a strange way, Vera, in her decisiveness, provided a modicum of security, someone who knew what she was doing, who spoke the language, who knew the territory. I could let go for a moment.

Granted, I was also ignoring all semblance of caution, and it occurred to me I was probably being led to a quiet place where this could end badly—the secondary crime scene—where there would be no one to save me. But I didn't care. It might even be for the best.

Let someone else do it.

Without turning back, Vera stuck a hand behind her, finding one of mine and, taking hold of it, she tugged me along wordlessly as she walked with purpose, propelling us through hordes of people, angling down cobblestoned streets until the colliding humanity diminished and the cacophony thinned, leaving us alone in front of a modest two-story walkup on a deserted street.

"Mi casa," she pronounced.

I imagined it probably wouldn't rise to more than a news brief:

## DISGRACED INVESTIGATIVE REPORTER
## FOUND DEAD IN MEXICO CITY

"Bueno," I said, retrieving one of my only handy Spanish phrases.

Up the narrow unlit staircase we went, Vera still not looking back at me, still connected to me by the umbilical cord of her fingers interlaced with mine. Maybe it would happen quickly. Perhaps, someone would emerge from the shadows and stab a hunting knife into my midsection, and I'd bleed out slowly, making something of a mess on the landing. I preferred a gunshot to the head. Quicker. Less painful. Neater, too. If we went with the hunting knife scenario, I was aware of how the body would go into instant shock, protecting me from feeling the

aftereffects of the initial attack. That was the benefit of inter-
viewing too many experts about too many bloody crime scenes.
But no one could say with certainty how death is experienced,
though I imagined there'd be a fleeting moment of recognition,
that this was it.

And then, a plunge into nothingness.

The door creaked open into a one-room dwelling. Letting
go of my hand for the first time since we'd met, Vera pulled a
cord from the ceiling, and a single light bulb illuminated no
one in the shadows.

Why didn't I feel relief?

While Vera slipped off her plastic heels in a clatter, I closed
the door behind me, pulled my cell phone from a back pocket,
and checked the bars: not much juice left. Barefoot, Vera
padded over to a small rusted stove and lit a flame under a
metal kettle. I glanced around for a place to sit and found only
one: a twin bed with a threadbare cover, tattered at the edges.
The small bed was shunted against a pockmarked white-washed
wall, under a wooden crucifix. Only then did I remember the
weight of the backpack digging into my shoulders. Maybe I'd
overpacked. Did I really need to bring my journal? Who was I
writing it for anyway?

Posterity?

Writing was a habit. Perhaps a bad habit. But a habit nonetheless. The act of placing words one in front of another, in a
specific order, with a certain rhythm built into the sentences,
like music on a blank page, brought a sense of order to the
chaotic mean tender world in which I lived, or rather, subsisted.

"Por favor sientate," Vera said, approaching me with a cup
of tea.

I got the idea, if not the words. Meekly, I complied, dropping my backpack on the grainy hardwood floor and lowering myself into a sitting position, sinking into the soft mattress, my back a bit too stiff to convey a sense of ease. Vera joined me, plopping down such that our hips were practically connected like conjoined twins.

"Mirame," she said.

I still didn't know what she was saying but I stole a glance at her, and in that split second, I realized she had a wide-open face with smooth edges, a shy smile bracketed by ripely molded cheeks. Long silky black hair cascaded down her bare soft shoulders. What I felt, though, was an overwhelming crush of fatigue. All I wanted to do was lie down and not wake up. I could barely keep my eyelids from drooping. Fearful of offending Vera, I suppressed a yawn but I couldn't prevent my tear ducts from watering. I feared she thought I was on the verge of weeping. Couldn't have that. I attempted a small smile that petered out.

"Bueno," I said.

I had, incidentally, no idea what was bueno, whether it was me, her, or our coarse surroundings. Vera seemed to know. Delicately, she placed the cup of tea on the barren floor. I traced her quiet movements, noticing a small detail, how meticulously she had painted her fingernails and toenails a matching dark shade of red, not missing a smidge. When I looked up, I found she was inspecting me. It was probably a good thing I couldn't speak Spanish and she didn't seem to know a stitch of English. Better not to converse; sometimes, chatter was overrated. Even more, better not to know what she was thinking, especially given the gentle look on her face.

Come to think of it, the tableau was just right. She couldn't offer a word of sympathy in a language I understood. I couldn't convey appreciation in her lexicon. None of those ridiculous sentiments. An added benefit: no internet. Vera's place was stripped down to its bare essence: a bed and a crucifix and little else. I was also feeling stripped down to my bare essence. Joe Gringo with nothing but the sparse possessions in my backpack: a toothbrush, a journal, and a change of clothing.

What's more, I was so cloaked in anonymity, I was practically infinite; there were millions of Joes, were she to try to Google me. Not just Joe Schmo, G.I. Joe, Joe Blow. I could be anyone, even someone who wasn't permanently stained with ruin. I could reimagine myself as someone with inherent worth.

I could be free falling.

My eyes struggled to remain open. They wanted to close oh so desperately, like when you're driving on an endless highway and the tapered line in the middle of the road mesmerizes you into a lull.

"Estas bien?" she murmured.

Vera came back into focus, and as I peered mutely at her in earnest for the first time, I was immediately struck by something about her big dark eyes, the symmetry of the precise part in her black hair, the soft luster of her smooth skin. She was, in that moment, incontestable.

Lifting her hand slowly, as if to alert me to its approach, so I wouldn't flinch like a rabbit with PTSD, Vera tenderly placed the tips of her lacquered fingernails on my perspiring forehead and brushed loose strands of wayward hair away from my stitched brow.

"Por que?" she asked quietly.

I continued to not bother to speak. Instead, I lowered my

head on a hardened pillow. I wanted to rest a moment. I needed to close my eyes for a second. I could see my chest rising and falling in regulated modulation. If she could give me a minute, we could resume this non-dance of ours. I'd even consider forking over a few pesos for the right to catch a quick catnap.

"No mas," I mumbled. "No mas."

Vera didn't need to do anything. Words weren't necessary. She'd already done quite enough. I could sense my mind unclenching.

There was something soothing about the prior moment, the tactile sensation of her hand in mine. The thought of it, the memory of the crease of her palm in mine, began to take me away, floating to another place, far from here, to an alcove of a tropical island of my imagination, remote and gleaming, where the tender sway of palm trees entranced me, a castaway from a shipwreck . . ..

# 26

When I awoke I realized, with considerable dismay, I was still here.

Not *here*, as in Vera's shorn dwelling. But *here*, as in the fallen world. No nefarious doings had occurred overnight in Vera's abode. In fact, I couldn't remember the last time I'd slept so soundly.

As I lifted my head, propping myself up on my elbows, I was forced to shield my eyes with a hand, so bright was the sun slanting through the single unshaded window in the one-room walkup.

I'd fallen asleep in my wrinkled clothes. My backpack sat where I had left it on the floor last night. My cellphone: kaput.

That's when I noticed I wasn't alone. With her back to

me, Vera stood barefoot by an unframed mirror, rhythmically brushing her long black hair.

Unexpected.

She hadn't snuck out during my slumber. She hadn't fled the scene. Why was she still here? Somehow, I had gotten it into my head that she had no reason to stay, even though this was her place.

Maybe she wanted to collect on what was owed. Granted, nothing of a carnal nature had transpired between us, except the hand holding, but I had lodged here overnight. Time to pay up, gringo.

Swinging my legs to the floor, I sat up unsteadily and reached into my pocket, retrieving my worn leather wallet. Leafing through it, I noticed nothing was missing from it, which struck me with a pang of guilt, that I had half expected Vera to have swiped a wad of cash from my wallet while I slept. Berating myself, I pulled out a small stack of pesos and placed them on the bed. But as Vera, hearing my rustling, turned toward me, she recoiled at the sight of the money.

"No, no," she scolded me.

"Por favor," I said, rising.

Vera marched over, pushed me back down onto the bed and shoved the money into my hand. Hurriedly, she moved to slip on a pair of sandals.

"Vamonos," she said impatiently.

Her body language spoke a universal language: that it was time to go. I'd evidently worn out my welcome. She was already ready, though garbed in a different dress, one of muted tones, without flash and verve. Even her face was unadorned, possessing none of the dazzle of last night's makeup. It was then that I noticed how pristine she appeared on a clear summer morning. Despite the frown written in paraphrase on her face, there wasn't a wrinkle marring her expression.

I wanted to thank her. I wanted to express gratitude for her act of kindness, for allowing me to sleep undisturbed for the first time since I couldn't remember when. But I couldn't find the words. I couldn't even remember the Spanish phrase for thank you, the most basic vocabulary. The distinct feeling was, I was akin to an infant without the knowledge of words to articulate a sentiment.

Instead, I reached into my backpack and groped about, until I found what I was looking for, wedged between a rolled-up T-shirt and a pair of crumpled jeans: a sweat-stained cap. I'm not sure why but, wordlessly, I handed the well-worn cap to Vera as a gift. She took it tentatively, not understanding the meaning.

"For you," I said.

Quizzically, she looked at the unprepossessing cap, then gaped at me, which was just as ragged, and nodded her head in assent.

"Gracias," she said, bowing her head.

Ah. Right. *Gracias.* How had I forgotten that word?

Vera placed the cap on the bed with the delicacy of a crown jewel being placed on a velvet display pillow, and she stepped toward the front door. Grabbing my backpack, I moved to leave.

"Adios," I said, thinking this was it.

But Vera offered me a puzzled look before shaking it off, and taking my hand, she led me out, down the narrow stairs into the hot daylight.

She wasn't quite done with me.

# 27

Vera didn't offer a hint of where we were going and I knew better than to ask along the way, even if I had known the words in Spanish.

Without the passage of words between us, we progressed on foot on a long journey from day into dusk, beyond paved roads and vrooming cars. Other marks of civilization fell away as did my desire or need to know where we were heading; did it really matter? My cellphone was drained, nothing more than a paperweight snug in my back pocket. Vera didn't deign to carry a smartphone. Throughout it all, she held my hand without interruption.

It occurred to me, I could have tried to explain to Vera that I had enough cash on me so that we could hail a taxi, or rent a car, or buy bus tickets—anything, really, to avoid an enforced march by foot. But the truth was, I didn't want to. This was good. I also had a sneaking suspicion Vera wouldn't have it any other way.

Early on, she pointed out a small body of crystalline water, where a poor family of four—by all appearances, a mother, a father, a son, and a daughter—splashed by the shore's edge. They weren't wearing bathing suits. Nothing so trite. They were wearing what they might wear anywhere on land: cutoff shorts and T-shirts. They had no beach toys, no tubes of suntan lotion. They just had each other.

Later, Vera gestured at a sparkling baseball field. It boasted emerald AstroTurf, night lights, and an electronic jumbo board. Billboards in the outfield screamed for Modelo Negra and other beer.

In the baseball field's shadow, across the street, a family of four—what looked like a mother and three emaciated children—squatted by the embers of a dying firepit. Vera headed straight for them, with me in tow. I had never seen the look before but I suspected what I detected on their faces was the mark of starvation. I didn't know what to do. Vera opened a small purse and handed the mother several bills. I did the same. I didn't know what to say. I glanced at Vera. She glanced back at me. There was a hardened look on her face, one speaking of earned knowledge. We moved on in silence.

Hours and miles and villages lapped us by, an odyssey of lives lived unobserved: children knocking an empty can, a chicken clucking and jutting, roaming free in a patch of desolation, where vegetation couldn't find a fertile field to grow, where water couldn't be ingested for fear of contamination.

It was getting late, and the dirt roads were becoming less distinct in the twilight, the soft glow of the sky still showing the way, and Vera kept moving with purpose, her hand sweaty in mine.

My mouth was parched, my stomach was grumbling, and I was beginning to wonder whether we'd ever stop—when Vera came to a halt.

We had arrived precisely nowhere. After a pause, Vera tugged me closer, waving a hand before us, drawing my attention to something beyond. I looked but saw nothing. She waved again impatiently as if to say: *Can't you see?* But all I could observe was the slab of rock on which we stood and a wide-open expanse.

"Mira," she said, gazing into the distance.

Peering ahead, I strained to see what Vera saw. But there was a distinct lack of observable terrain—no trees before us, no bushes—nothing but an infinite stretch of atmosphere and a smattering of clouds, through which the sun was descending, joining with the horizon, creating a vast cavass of pink against cerulean sky.

That's when I got it. The sky. The setting sun. That was it. That's what Vera was trying to alert me to. It wasn't an event. There were no pyrotechnics. It was just what was right before us, seen but unseen.

But what of it?

Vera explained without explanation, falling to her knees. She nodded at me to do the same. I did without protest. She folded her hands in a tent of prayer and bent her head down in supplication.

Before I could do the same—I was preoccupied watching

her—Vera nudged me to get going. I didn't have the heart—or the words—to tell her I wasn't like her, I didn't have the gift of belief, I didn't have the strength of faith. So, I got going. I folded my hands and bowed my head, feeling like a fool.

Out of the corner of one eye, I observed Vera close her eyes and emit hushed words I couldn't quite discern. My prayer—well, it wasn't a prayer but a random wish—was that we would get to wherever we were heading soon. I was famished. A hope lurked beyond that wish, a hope that I would find what I was looking for, that this excursion into the heart of Mexico wasn't sheer folly.

Pausing from her prayer, Vera peeked at me, startled by my opened eyes, and took an aggravated intake of breath. With exaggeration, she blinked repeatedly—until I got the message, to close my eyes—which I did with some reluctance. I mean, I could only go so far with this charade. But she insisted, and there it was.

Now, eyes shut, I was in the dark. Couldn't see a thing. I could only make out the vague wanderings of her Spanish prayer, punctuated by a clarion call to Jesus. Had she understood any English, I would've asked Vera, even if that wasn't her real name: Why now? Why here? What had prompted this unscheduled stop on a rock in the deserted countryside?

But we couldn't speak, not with a semblance of understanding, and so I simply complied, remaining silent on my knees, hands folded, with my eyes shuttered, until I found myself induced into a preternatural calm, owing to the rare instance of doing absolutely nothing.

It took me a moment to realize Vera had stopped praying. Cautiously, I opened my eyes. She was already on her feet, smiling at me beatifically, a hand outstretched, as she said, "Vamos."

# 28

It was nearing nightfall when a makeshift hut came into view, illuminated from within by the light of a candle. Vera knocked thrice, and a moment later, the wooden front door burst open.

A bearded man emerged. Recognizing Vera, he enfolded her in a tight embrace as a rush of warm words crisscrossed between them.

During the exchange, Vera nodded in my direction, lowered her voice, as if to avoid being overheard, and said "Joe" something-something, to which the bearded man, considerably older than Vera, tutted back at her, saying, "Si, si," as if he understood everything there was to understand.

"So, you meet my sister, Vera?" he turned to ask me in clipped English.

Her real name? *"Sister?"* I replied in slight astonishment. They looked nothing alike.

The bearded man ignored my question to his question. "Welcome," he said solemnly, ushering us, with an extended arm, into his thatched hut.

We were instantly greeted by the open arms of a harried woman—presumably his wife—with cotton sleeves folded up to her elbows. A gaggle of small children followed suit, hugging Vera's legs and piling into mine.

Almost imperceptibly, Vera slipped a wad of pesos into the bearded man's hand.

What was that about? The question overlapped with a din of voices.

"Come, come," he insisted.

It appeared we had intruded on the tail end of their dinner: wooden plates of rice and beans and boiled fish. But drawing up chairs for Vera and me, we were seated with the rest of the family around a small rectangular wooden table. Vera's brother held up a gnarled hand, calling for our attention.

"Forgive me," he said, sitting at the head of the table. "My English, not so good. I am fisherman. Vera tell me you good man. You eat. But first, we do something. We hold hand like this."

And he showed and we did. "And we pray," he added.

I was tempted to note that Vera and I had already performed this act of supplication not long before arriving here. Instead, out of politeness, I waited. I could do it again. But nothing happened. They were all looking at me expectantly—even the children, and I counted five of them, all smiling broadly, each looking entirely different than the others, except for their eyes, which were wide and clear, hair flung in every direction. None could've been older than seven.

"Por favor," said their mother, tapping me lightly on the hand.

Not understanding, I looked to Vera for guidance, and she tilted her chin at her brother, spinning out words of direction quickly, which prompted him to say, "Ah." Rising, he moved off to a wooden side table and retrieved a worn Bible, handing it to me.

"Please," he said.

The page was already laid open before me. I glanced at Vera for approval: *Me?*

She smiled as if to say: Yes, you.

That's when I noticed the Bible carried an English translation of the Spanish version on the page opposite it. No excuse. I cleared my throat, a bit uncomfortably, not feeling qualified to speak these words. But I did:

Our Father in heaven
    Hallowed be your name.

Your kingdom come,
    your will be done,
      on earth as it is in heaven.

Give us this day our daily bread,
    and forgive us our debts,
      as we also have forgiven our debtors.

And lead us not into temptation,
    but deliver us from evil.

The lack of a reaction caused me to look up at an array of faces.

*What?*

Grasping for an acknowledgment, I turned to Vera, who, in meeting my eyes with the piercing of hers, appeared to understand that I had finished the prayer.

"Amen," she said, cuing the rest.

There it was: *Amen.* The word cascaded around the table from one to another. Amen, amen, amen, amen, amen, amen, amen. As it turned out, the word was the same in Spanish as it was in English.

"Don't worry," Vera's bearded brother said from across the table. "Today, you eat. Tonight, you sleep. Tomorrow, I take you."

Where wasn't an issue. At the moment, it didn't matter. All that I cared about was how, in the first forkful of food I ladled into my hungry mouth, I had just tasted the most delectable rice and beans and boiled fish ever.

# 29

The following morning, still and peaceful, came soon enough, too soon, but here it was, and before I could commit to memory all that I had witnessed the night before—the sunset, wind-chimes clinking, laughter, prayer, fellowship, you name it—I found myself being ushered into a dilapidated taxi, a makeshift contraption, the kind that emitted worrisome conks from the tailpipe that would auger a forced retirement.

The taxi car door shut unceremoniously.

By the dirt road, Vera was standing outside the taxi, stone faced in profile.

She refused to look in my direction, shrouding her expression from me. She folded her arms tightly, as if she were precariously holding the machinery—her assembled pieces—together.

"Pablo take you," Vera's brother told me, breaking the silence, standing next to her, leaning into the open window, and patting me on the back. "Pablo know all roads. He my friend. He speak English good."

At that endorsement, Pablo, in the driver's seat, grinned toothily at me via the rearview mirror, with one of his eyes off-kilter from the other, and away we rattled, as I craned my head back to catch a final glimpse of Vera, like a mirage undulating in the morning summer heat.

"Where to, chief?" Pablo asked cheerfully.

"Don't know," I grumbled, settling into the busted vinyl backseat.

"Lost?" he asked, taking another look at me in the rearview mirror.

"That's one way of putting it," I offered stingily.

It was the only way of putting it. Strictly speaking, we were somewhere on the outskirts of Mexico City. Couldn't have gotten that far on foot, especially in less than twenty-four hours.

But metaphorically speaking, I was utterly lost. I had no idea where I was. I didn't know where I was going. I didn't even know who I was anymore, or whether there was any point to this windmill-tilting pursuit; I had to remind myself the point was to find Maggie's father, to make sense of the insensible.

"Let's head back to Mexico City," I said morosely.

"Ten-four, chief." Pablo winked at me from the rearview mirror.

Just like that, I was making an arcing circle, heading back from whence I came. An endless loop. What had been the point? Mine was too meager of an understanding. I lacked the inherent capacity to see the grand design in my own distended life, if there ever was one. (And there wasn't.) I was wound up too much in my own head, inoculated from the essential survival skills of intuition, common sense, and the incumbent fear of the unknown.

"Hey, chief," Pablo called out. "Whaddaya wanna do when we get to Mexico City?"

"Just drive around," I said without a plan.

"No problem," he nodded.

I'd have to improvise. Actually, more likely, I'd have to give up the pursuit of the whereabouts of Maggie's father. The only problem was, from my vantage point, I didn't know how to let go.

# 30

Pablo kept up a steady stream of chatter from the driver's seat of the taxi, most of which I only vaguely followed, grunting in assent at the loose ends of his run-on conjugated sentences.

"Right," I said, hand on chin.

That tended to be the appropriate response to almost anything Pablo put out in the space between us—him up front, behind the wheel, navigating us back to civilization; me, ensconced in the back seat, brooding over the prospect of writing my next letter to Maggie, telling her I had failed her, that I couldn't track down her father in Mexico.

"And so there I was," Pablo exclaimed, apparently reaching a crescendo to whatever intricate tale with which he was regaling me.

"Ah," I offered in reply.

The truth was, I had failed myself. The great unemployed investigative reporter wasn't so great, not nearly. Just unemployed and ruined. I was a victim of my own hubris, thinking I could do the impossible, despite Maggie's protestations, telling me to forget about the whole mess. My own vanity compelled me to barrel forth, recklessly plowing into my present circumstances, in inevitable declension: broke, broken, unfixable.

"But then," Pablo said, raising a finger, interrupting my self-flagellation.

He didn't finish his sentence. He was waiting for an audience.

I complied: "What happened?"

"Glad you asked," he said, craning over his shoulder to check my pulse as displayed on my non-expressive face. For a split second, I worried he wasn't paying any attention to the road spread before us, one hand on the steering wheel. But the ambition faded.

"What happened was," he continued, turning back to the road, "a rock fell."

"A rock?"

"Si, a rock."

A rock didn't help. I didn't have enough information. I couldn't relocate the conversation based on that one solitary thread.

"I don't understand," I admitted.

"Me neither," Pablo said, evincing for the first time a pit of unsubmerged sadness. He let a long moment pass unattended, a vacant stretch of road unwinding. *Was that an eagle or a vulture swooping above us?*

"A rock," Pablo said, staring ahead. "It fell by itself. It was just time for the rock to fall. Not the day before, or the day after. It happened at the exact time it was supposed to happen."

Not wanting to know what happened, I asked, "What happened?"

"That morning, my beloved was making huevos rancheros," he said in perfect English. "Just like always. But after, she forgot her scarf as she stepped outside. She returned to get it. A scarf. A decoration. A thing she didn't need. That took maybe three seconds. That might've been enough. The forgetting, the getting the scarf. She walked the same road she always took to the village. It was always the same. Except for the rock, when it fell."

Pablo paused, unable to articulate the tragedy that befell his beloved.

"After she was gone," he finally said, "I was blinded by a primitive rage I cannot describe. I fled from my village, from my life, from my suffering. I tried to cross the border. Si, I'm what you gringos call a wetback. But not for long. I was caught right away. I was never good at such things, sneaking around. They put me in an Immigration Detention Center. You know what that is, right? It's a fancy name for a prison. But there was nothing fancy about this place. On my first day, I was beaten by gangbangers. Why? No reason. I lost sight in my left eye. But don't worry. I can still see the road. You only need one good eye to see what's ahead. No? I was supposed to be—what's the word? Deported. Within forty-eight hours. But when I lost sight in the left eye, I lost two months in prison. When I was released, I was dumped off in Tijuana, dazed. Adios, Amigo. I was still wearing the dirty gray sweats they had put on me in prison. Street vendors sold chewing gum and hotdogs. Street walkers sold their bodies. I had nothing to sell. Therefore, I had no money. No phone. All I had was what I found: a side street, where I fell asleep on concrete. Si, it happened without my noticing: I became homeless. A beggar, you call it. I learned a hard lesson. What happened to me can happen to anyone, the destruction, the desolation. Before long, I was starving to death. It didn't take much time before I carried the stench of human waste wherever I went. I didn't want to live. I wasn't living. I was dying little by little. And that's when it happened."

"Yes?"

"I heard a voice."

"A voice?" I asked, reflexively thinking of the voice I had heard.

"Si, a voice," he said.

I was reminded of what that indeterminate voice had whispered to me: *Look. Go.*

"What did the voice say?" I asked, not daring to mention my own.

Pablo said, "'Get up.'"

"Get up?"

"Si. 'Get up.' In Spanish, of course. Levantate."

"That's it?"

"Si, God speaks Spanish, of course," Pablo said. "Who was I to argue? So, I got up, covered in grime and filth. I stumbled. I was dizzy. My teeth were loose and my gums ached. I was weak. My face was stained with tears and boils. I was like a leper, an outcast."

"Where did you go?"

"I don't know," Pablo said, shifting to the present tense, as if he was there now, experiencing it all over. "I just start walking south. I keep walking until I can't. Then I sleep on the side of the road. I rummage through garbage for scraps of rotten lettuce, spoiled meat, cockroaches, things you can't imagine. I wake up and begin to walk again, day after day. The pain in my legs is so great, like daggers mocking me. You can't recognize me, the long beard, the wild hair caked with mud, the death in my eyes. Muerte. I lose track of days and nights. I lose the ability to speak. My mind is lost in a maze of agony and confusion. I think it will never end—until I see a road sign point the way: Chihuahua.

"Somehow, I make it there, a city crowded and alive. My one good eye opens a little wider. I realize I'm going somewhere. Not here. But somewhere else. Farther south. There is a destination. I keep going. I keep walking. I keep moving for days and weeks—maybe months. I'm not sure. Once, I think I see my beloved in front of me on the road. She waves, before vanishing.

"How do you say? A delusion? An illusion? I can't remember which."

I was about to reply but Pablo didn't wait for an answer.

"Finally, one day, I can walk no more. I collapse. I crawl on my hands and knees, the ribs of my chest scraping against the dirt. But I stop moving. There is nothing left. This is it. I wait to die. That's when I hear a voice—a different voice. I look up, squinting into the blinding sun, and there she is: Vera. I don't know who she is. Maybe an angel, I think. Then, black. Nothing. The next thing I remember, she is placing a wet cloth on my forehead. She lifts my head to drink water. She prays for me. When I have enough strength, she brings me to her brother's village."

I don't know why but I asked, "Is he really her brother?"

Pablo eyed me over his shoulder. "No, not technically," he decided to say. "Vera was adopted."

The reveal wasn't simply that she wasn't the bearded man's sister. What threw me for a loop was that she didn't take the money I had offered to her. She had let me sleep in peace. She had saved Pablo. She took both of us at different times to this remote village, to be salvaged. She had given money to the bearded man who wasn't her brother. Had I been all wrong about what I assumed about her? But this question didn't allow Pablo to finish telling his story.

"What happened next?" I asked.

Pablo's voice quivered in a slight betrayal of rising emotion; he cleared his throat to steady himself.

"God wasn't finished with me," he said. "He had other plans for me."

There was no point in disabusing Pablo of his notion of fate. It worked for him. Besides, here he was, obviously recovered, thriving enough to operate his own taxi, even with one good eye. I'd reserve my skepticism for myself. That, by the way, explained my hesitation to respond, overcome as I was by the enormity of Pablo's epic story. I was left with too many questions but did not feel worthy to ask them. Pablo saved me from the awkwardness.

"Small problem, chief," he said in a different voice, relaxed.

"Yes?"

"We're lost," he said breezily.

My first instinct was to look inward, and I realized no one would miss me if I got lost for good. Okay, maybe Tally. But she had to. She was related by blood. There was no one else to worry where I had disappeared to, no one to wonder why I hadn't called or answered repeated messages. My father: Locked up for good. Mom: Long gone. Maggie? She had her own problems behind bars, leaving aside that we'd never even met, and she had another decade to go before she'd get out. Owing to my travels of late, it had been weeks since we'd corresponded by mail, Maggie and I, and who knew where that left us? Not that there was an us in the first place—except in my daydreams. The shape of Maggie's face was already beginning to fade; I couldn't quite see the outline anymore. I was losing the thread of Maggie. What was left was more of a lingering feeling—an unspecified longing. I knew what was there, inherent in Maggie, was painfully beautiful. I just couldn't describe it now.

The unvarnished truth—pushing aside all distractions—was that I was the kind of Average Joe who, in a permanent state of disgrace, would likely be discovered one day in a musty apartment, sprawled out on a futon, a decomposed body, a New York affliction.

Second instinct: I looked around, and it dawned on me that, caught up in Pablo's tale, not paying attention, we had somehow managed to get ourselves stuck in a snarl of minor traffic apparently on the outskirts of Mexico City.

"Do you have GPS?" I asked.

"GPS?"

"A map?"

"Only in my head," Pablo said, tapping his temple with a stubby finger.

"How do you know where to go?"

"It's all in here." He knocked on his temple again confidently. "I know all these roads—how do you say?—like the back of my head."

"*Hand*," I corrected the idiom. "Like the back of your hand."

"Hand—head, same thing," he said. "Except these roads. Don't know them at all. Have no idea where we are."

Another option: I began to pull out my phone but halted, recalling it was dead.

"What now?" I asked.

"We wait," Pablo said peacefully.

"For what?"

"For a sign."

"You mean, we wait for a sign from above?" I asked dubiously.

"Why not?" Pablo said, shrugging.

Because I didn't believe. Because it was ludicrous. Because—

"There," Pablo exclaimed, pointing.

That didn't take long.

He wasn't pointing up. He was pointing sideways. I indulged him, looking in that direction, through the thicket of traffic, in the near distance. And, lo and behold, there was indeed a sign:

## SAN MIGUEL DE ALLENDE
### 275 KM

Not exactly a sign from above, but a sign nonetheless.

"See?" Pablo was grinning again in the rearview mirror. I wasn't sure whether he was asking a question or pronouncing a miracle.

"See what?" I replied.

"San Miguel."

"What about it?"

"Just north of us," he said.

"How far is it?"

"A little over three hours," he said almost apologetically.

"The way I drive, maybe closer to two."

"What's there?" I asked, unconvinced.

"Not much," Pablo admitted. "They don't even have stop signs or stoplights there."

"Oh."

"Nothing but balloon vendors," he continued dismissively. "And doors."

"Doors?"

"People's front doors," he said. "In San Miguel, it's a thing. Homes come with colorful doors. You will find doorknockers in the shape of lizards. Some doors are—how do you say? Colonial. The doors are sacred passages from outside to inside."

"Hm," I offered weakly. San Miguel sounded like a tourist's haven.

"Lot of tourists," Pablo confirmed, as if reading my thoughts.

"Hm." I nodded.

"Lots of artists," he added.

"Hm," I grunted.

"Lots of people like you," he persisted.

"Like me?"

"Gringos," he clarified. "Americanos. *Americans.*"

Perking up, I rewound Enos's words in my head, recalling the recent conversation back at his shack in Skiatook, about his old friend, Maggie's father: *Smack dab in the middle. Hidden in plain sight.*

A hunch: Luke could be hiding there.

"Where exactly in Mexico," I asked, "is San Miguel?"

"Pretty much in the middle of the map," Pablo said. "Why you ask?"

It was a bit of a stretch. Hardly enough to hang your hat

on. But what else did I have? In another truism of the life of the investigative reporter—based on a lesson imparted by a far greater journalist than I ever was, the unblinking editor who let me go when it all fell apart—it was vital to trust your instincts.

Sitting up straight in the back of the cab, I said, "Let's go."

# 31

When Pablo and I rumbled into San Miguel that afternoon, my relentless ruminations obscured the aesthetics of the pretty place. I barely noticed the church steeples, the arched columns, and those front doors—radiating bright yellow and green and orange. I took little heed of the narrow winding cobbled streets and the retirees, lugging stylish shopping bags. I was nearly oblivious to the wreath of mountain vistas encompassing us from a distance.

Pablo had mercifully parked the wheezing car in a village square, and we had set forth on foot, the two of us, as I stopped people at random to ask whether they had seen a man, an American now in his fifties, who once looked like the image in a frazzled old picture, Luke as a young man, crooked grin and all.

The question drew baffled looks. Sometimes, it wasn't just the oddity of the question itself. Often, they didn't understand my English. Pablo would translate in Spanish. Then they would recoil in confusion: What kind of question was *that*? Of course, they had no idea who I was searching for. How could anyone peer at a thirty-year-old photo and extrapolate what the person would appear like today? It was the height of absurdity, and the consistent utterances I fielded took on the steady drumbeat of a rhythmic cadence, a forced march to nowhere: No. No. No. No. No. No. No. Another pithy word with the same meaning in English as in Spanish, albeit with a slightly different accent.

Amid my repeated failures, Pablo was the picture of patience, standing beside me, head bowed, scuffling. But I couldn't continue to subject him to my pointless pursuit. With the gradual decline of the sun in the dying day, I knew it was time to let him go. He faced a long drive back home. In my inimical bumbling way, I tried to thank him, handing him a sweaty wad of uncounted cash. He accepted it amiably, no argument. He didn't try to persuade me to let him stay with me. He didn't make any effort to stop me from the insanity of my hunt. All Pablo did was place a rough hand on my shoulder, look at me with his one good eye, and say, "This is your path, chief. I have faith you will find what you are looking for. Or it will find you. God is with you."

Flinching, I said nothing in return. What I was thinking, as he clattered off in his old jalopy, was that the only thing with me was profound gnawing doubt. And my plan, which I began executing almost immediately and over the next two days, was to wash away the persistent unease, performing my ablutions in a dank bar.

# 32

On my third day in San Miguel, I stopped asking people on the streets about the frayed photo of Luke after I was confronted by one complete stranger who scowled at me and sputtered impatiently: "You asked me that question already, hombre."

Si. I was losing track of the people whom I didn't know.

Properly chastened, I retreated to the gringo bar tucked away under my cold water flat, a one-room hovel with a clinking sink faucet.

A hand—mine, apparently—barely propped up my slumping face, while I whittled away that afternoon at the bar, lifting an index finger every so often, cuing the bartender to fill my glass with another shot of tequila.

In brief: I was attempting to drink myself into oblivion,

an insulated place built with the deleterious effects of a potent concoction of prescription pills past their expiration date.

Woozy, I allowed my mind to wander to Maggie. What was she doing? Reading a campy romance novel? Scrapbooking? Crocheting? The thread that connected us to each other was thinning; an occasional letter couldn't harness Maggie's heart, even if mine was already drawn. It needed her. No. That wasn't it. It needed the *idea* of her. An illusion or, to borrow a Pablo malapropism, a delusion. Maybe Maggie was merely a mirage, just as Pablo's beloved had become to him, in the aftermath, after she appeared to him on his road to restoration.

My heart was so bereft of comfort and caresses, it swelled at just the notion of a theoretical possibility of something, a phrase, an expression, a name. *Maggie.* Marinated as I was in a bottle of tequila, I imagined the day when Maggie is set free, and I'm waiting at the prison gate, African daisies in hand. Don't know why I picked those. Could be tomorrow. Or a decade from now. It doesn't matter. Because I've waited. As she emerges, she hesitates, not sure who I am. But before I can say, she intuitively knows and runs to embrace me—a hug that almost barrels me over. I pick up a distinct scent on her neck, that of fresh soap—Irish Spring—and it is the most wonderful scent I've ever inhaled. Wetness sprinkles my neck as Maggie sheds tears of joy. I want to tell her something but the words can't get out. I can't tell her about the rented RV parked behind us. I can't manage to explain how I've planned a trip that will take us along the west coast, down California State Route 1, to Big Sur. *There will be time,* I tell myself. Don't rush it. Let her breathe.

I could almost picture the RV rumbling down the glistening unencumbered highway, me at the wheel, the passenger window wide open, Maggie's hair flying free in the breeze. I was almost smiling wistfully into the distorted image of myself in an empty tequila shot glass, enthralled by what could come, the simplicity of the daydream, the endless possibilities it suggested, when the moving picture in my mind was interrupted by a voice with a slight twang:

"Hey, buddy."

Roused from my stupor, I peered around, through a dim haze, at a sturdy older man who stood by my bar stool, and I girded myself to inform him I was no buddy of his when I registered something familiar about his grin.

*Luke?*

"I know what you're looking for," he leaned in, out of earshot.

"You do, do you?" I slurred.

"Joe, right?"

"Bingo," I crowed.

"It's a small town," he said with a drawl. "Word gets around. There are only so many gringos showin' an old photo tryin' to find someone who don't look like that picture no more."

"It's complicated," I mumbled.

"We expats don't all look alike," he said. "But we just about all know each other."

"That right?" I was trying to shake the murky cobwebs from my head.

"Come with me," he said, moving to leave, without looking back.

"Where're we going?" I said, stumbling off my barstool.

He didn't say. I didn't ask again. Sometimes, you find what you're looking for precisely when you're not looking for it anymore.

# 33

I didn't find Luke. He found me.

The mysterious man at the bar casually mentioned he was the object of my search while he took me in his open-air Jeep on a short excursion to the outskirts of San Miguel. Along the way, rumbling on roads carved out of dirt, there was no mention of Maggie, his daughter. I wasn't even sure he knew of her existence; she had, after all, been born after his disappearance. He just made a pronouncement in passing: "Yes, I'm Luke."

As dusk settled in, he pulled up to the entrance of a modest ranch, and I couldn't help but wonder why he was doing this, identifying himself, exposing himself after decades in hiding. Perhaps I should've been worried. But I was long past that extraneous emotion.

Pablo's prophesy returned to me: *You will find what you are looking for. Or it will find you.* No doubt, Pablo would've credited the supernatural for helping me find what I was looking for. I accounted for it by acknowledging my dumb luck. Sometimes, these things happen. Eventually, by dint of brute-force effort, you break through. Or bump into it. No need to impose a grand design on it.

Right?

That I wasn't quite convinced unsettled me. Maybe there was something to Pablo's mumbo jumbo. After all the futile searching, after all the lashing doubts, I didn't quite know what to make of what I absorbed as Luke opened the front door of his home, and I stepped into the foyer.

What struck me immediately was how the life Luke led was remarkable in its ordinariness: a cluster of framed family pictures. A potted plant. A flat-screen TV. The place was so generic in its middle-class comfort, it gave off the air of any cookie-cutter American suburban dwelling; it just happened to be a home plopped down in the middle of Mexico.

Without formalities, Luke settled into a wingback chair in his living room and gestured for me to sit on a leather couch catty-corner to him.

"I have a family," he began evenly, "and I will do anythin' to protect 'em, including shooting you dead right here right now."

With that indelicate introduction, Luke removed a rather large semiautomatic weapon from behind him and rested the firearm in his lap.

"Fair enough," I said unmoved.

"I have a beautiful wife," he continued with a trace of an Oklahoma twang. "We've been married for near thirty years, and we have two grown sons. I'm retired, and you should know I mind my own business."

I wasn't sure why I should know that. I merely nodded my head.

"So, mister, tell me one thing," he said. "Are you with them?" "*Them?*"

"You know who I'm talking about," he drawled. "The cartel."

Without meaning to, I guffawed incredulously: "No."

"That funny to you?" Luke sneered, clasping his semiautomatic.

With a straight face, I asked, "Do I look like I'm with the cartel?"

Luke shook his head: "You look like you're one step removed from a hobo."

He betrayed his age with that remark. Who said hobo anymore? Then again, I betrayed myself with my bedraggled beard, which had resumed its encroachment over my gaunt face. Or was it the weary hopelessness in my bloodshot eyes that betrayed me?

"I'm here because of Maggie," I said.

"Maggie?"

"Your daughter."

"Got you there, mister," Luke said. "I don't have no daughter."

"Actually," I said, "you do."

Luke loosened his grip on the gun; I could sense he was struggling to process the implications of what I had just said. I relieved him of the monumental effort, explaining the whole shebang: how I had encountered Maggie and learned of her mother's pregnancy, what Enos had confided in me about the fake car collision all those years ago and the tragedy of Maggie's incarceration. The only thing I didn't tell Luke was about my own misery and destruction. Not that he would've cared; it was beside the point.

Luke didn't say a word. I'm not sure he breathed during what felt like a soliloquy I'd memorized. It looked like he was in the grip of a coming seizure until he uttered a single word with shaky reverence, as if testing out an unfamiliar word, unwrapped.

"Maggie."

"Now," I said when I got him up to speed, "it's your turn. How'd you end up here?"

Agitated, Luke rose and began to pace. He didn't bother to hold the gun, which he left resting on the cushion of the wingback chair. I guess I had proven myself not to be enough of an imminent threat.

So, it was true: As he began to wrestle with the narrative of the winding past, Luke let it be known he had indeed been a drug runner at the U.S.-Mexican border and recklessly absconded with boatloads of cartel cash. He had in fact faked his own death. His old friend Enos had been true to his word about the staged car wreck and the payoffs to the sheriff's deputy and the coroner and the urn with the squirrel's ashes.

"Who," I interrupted, "scrubbed down your truck?"

"What?" he responded without understanding.

"Your truck was found parked by the pier on South Padre Island in immaculate shape."

"Hm," Luke said, pondering that newly raised fact with raised eyebrows. "Suppose the cartel wanted to clean up any loose ends."

"And why," I asked, "would the cartel leave Enos alone?"

Luke stopped pacing. "Only one possible reason," he said, working it out as he spoke. "Enos didn't steal no money from no cartel. That much, I'm sure you could tell from the way that ol' geezer lives. Cheap as a cardboard box. But Enos was with me when I died—at least, that's what the cartel thought when they figured I was killed in that mangled car wreck thirty years ago."

"Meaning what?" I asked.

"Meaning, the cartel reckoned Enos had a debt to pay. My debt. Just because he was with me. They'da been suspicious he was in on it. He'da been responsible to pay back every penny of what I stole, poor soul."

Despite his description of Enos as the unintended patsy of the ill-gotten goods, Luke showed little remorse for having placed his old friend in such a financial bind. I couldn't resist: "How much money are we talking about?"

Luke eyed me coldly. "Enough," he said before shifting gears. "The point is, Enos would have to keep working for the cartel until the debt was paid off."

"What kind of work?" I asked, though I had a pretty good idea of what it entailed.

"Drug running," Luke said. "What else?"

"Enos still on the cartel's payroll?"

"Based on the amount of money involved, I'd imagine so," Luke said. "That's how these things work."

Luke plunked himself back in his wingback chair and lit a cigar, letting it all sink in. Now it was my turn to rise and pace in agitation. I still couldn't quite put all the pieces together.

"What about Maggie?" I asked.

"What about her?" He let out a big billow of smoke, clouding his presence.

"What does her case have to do with you?"

Luke gave me a querulous look: "Not a thing."

There was no room for interpretation. Only one thing had been cleared up: the death and undeath of Luke. But what had befallen Maggie—the tragedy of her incarceration and the loss of her daughter Mary—had nothing to do with Luke and his strange circumstances. Somehow, I had allowed the two different tracks—the supposed death of Maggie's father and her own case—to merge into one, when they were unrelated and had always been. How in the world had I ever thought those two disparate events were connected? I couldn't remember the origins of that theory. In my need for cohesion, I had been searching for a connection where there wasn't one: Luke's death and Maggie's imprisonment. I had been looking for internal logic, where A leads to B, which is followed by C, when in reality it doesn't work that way; life is a disorderly mess in 3D, where A leads to X, before circling back to D for no rotten reason.

By the time I glanced back at Luke, I could surmise he'd been surveying me as I was trying to untangle the strands of things I couldn't quite grasp.

"Anything else?" he asked, growing impatient, tamping out his cigar well before it was reduced to a stub.

"One last thing," I said. "There was an old man I met on South Padre Island. He walked with a cane. Told me he had a bad knee. And he had an old scar he tried to hide over his left eyebrow."

"Ah," Luke said.

"Know who he is?"

"Sounds like the sheriff's deputy," he said. "As it happened, he needed a touch of convincing before he agreed to report my death as a traffic fatality way back when. But don't you worry. Enos and I made it worth his while, financially speaking."

Made sense. The old man with the cane had been quite observant—perhaps too observant. Not surprising for a retired member of law enforcement.

"He needed convincing?"

"A bit of persuasion," Luke said, "involving a blunt force object to his knee and forehead."

Luke chuckled as if remembering an old joke. Still a fanged-tooth panther, this one.

"You know," I said, wondering whether I should say the words as they came out, "Maggie would sure like to meet her father."

Use of the third-person pronoun: father instead of you; better to ease into it than to employ the second-person right away.

Luke stood a little too quickly.

"I mean," I added, "she's always wondered about her father."

Luke moved to the front door.

"She's a good woman," I continued, trailing after him, ratcheting up the sales pitch.

Luke opened the door.

"She's been through a lot," I said, stopping at the threshold.

Luke turned back. "Listen," he said, scratching his chin. "I got a life here."

Other members of it were nowhere to be seen—not his wife, nor his grown sons. Luke didn't bother to caution me to keep my mouth shut, though this would've been about the right time to throw that into the mix. Instead, he asked offhand, "You got I.D.?"

"Excuse me?"

"A driver's license will do," he said.

I complied, fishing it out of my wallet. With his phone, Luke took a snapshot of my license; not much of a picture. That was me before the destruction, another person, barely recognizable now. The photo he took was just insurance. Luke knew who I was. But he knew there was no chance of me yapping. I was with Maggie, and he was, despite his reticence to meet her, still connected to her, if only biologically, and I think he knew instinctively, because he survived on those atavistic impulses, that I would never reveal him.

"This is just a bad situation," he said, reaching in his pocket, groping for his car keys. "And I can't undo what's been done."

I'd hit a dead end. I would of course write to Maggie to let her know about her father. It was the least I could do. She'd want to know. But I was left dispossessed. Luke didn't want to have anything to do with his daughter. Even worse, Maggie was still locked up for a crime I was convinced she hadn't committed.

# 34

Dear Joe,

It's okay, everything you found out in Mexico, all of it. I'm just glad to know my biological father is alive and well, even if he doesn't have the gumption to want to meet me. I get it.

To be honest, I'm even more relieved to know you got home safely.

I have to admit, it's strange to think I have two grown brothers I've never met, half-brothers but brothers still. I wonder what they look like. I wonder if they are a little like me.

By the way, it might be better if you don't mention any of this to my mama—about my father being alive and all. You know how she can be. She's liable to get a bit cantankerous. No need to get her all riled up for no reason. It is what it is.

Well, I suppose this is the end of the line, right? You've done everything you can do and more, and I'm forever grateful. The fact is, my father is who he is and I am where

I am. Hard to ever forget that. People around here like to keep reminding you, what with all the rules and regulations.

Sometimes I wonder whether I'd know how to act on the outside. What I mean is, I can't do anything without permission inside here. That's ten solid years of asking for the right to take a shower. You know what I mean? I'm not sure I'd know how to be once I get out of here ten years from now. Hard to picture it.

All I can do is pray. That's what I do every day. I am unwavering in my faith in God. I believe there will be a restoration. I believe there will be a path forward. I believe there will be another way. I don't know what it is yet, but I know it's coming.

Take care of yourself, Joe.

Blessings,

Maggie

P.S. Don't forget to get a dog.

# 35

Crouched in a fetal position, I was shivering but not chilly. I was but couldn't be. It was still the dead of summer, and I was holed up in the box of my stifling apartment in New York, the one for which I had recently received an eviction notice. I rolled over on the futon, in a sweaty tangle of sheets, unable to rise, my head pounding, taking another glance at Maggie's last letter. It sounded like a goodbye. Permanent. Her missive was kind of like getting kicked out of my apartment, or losing my life as I knew it. None of it could be mended. Inexorable.

Weeks had seeped by, uneventful and viscous, while I throttled myself with a steady diet of drink and prescription drugs. My only salve. The plunge seemed bottomless, a relentless spiral that wracked my body, dulled my senses, and submerged me in a vague consciousness that allowed for no sharp-edged realities or truths.

Disembodied images flashed in the interstices of my mind-altered state: Pablo and his one good eye, navigating dusty backroads. Vera and her unwillingness to face me when I departed that village in Mexico. Luke and his unfinished cigar. And Maggie.

Especially Maggie.

I couldn't get up. I couldn't move. I couldn't do anything. There was no beginning, no end, no way out. I was just broken and listless, unable or unwilling to act, speak, or emote. With my eyes shut tightly against the sunbeams of the rising day, I wondered whether I was imagining it all, thinking perhaps it was just a nightmare, or an alternate reality, just a figment of my imagination.

Maybe my mind was playing tricks on me. Was it possible I wasn't here? Could it be that what I thought had happened didn't? There was nothing more to do. I only waited. Not even waiting. Didn't even do that. I merely was. I'd given up; not just on Maggie's case, I'd given up on myself, the semblance of a feeble effort.

Days-old Chinese food sat sprouting spores on the kitchen counter. I'd lost my appetite as evidenced by my hollowed-out cheeks. I'd run out of clean clothing eons ago. I hadn't charged my phone when it ran out of juice—not that there was anyone calling, except spunky telemarketers, which only made things worse. My lips were parched. I was thirsty—dehydrated—but couldn't muster the ambition to rise and fetch a dirty glass of water.

Too far away.

A single tear formed at the narrowed edge of my right eye.

It hovered there, threatening to fall, on the precipice, but didn't.

I even failed at that. I felt like laughing but was too tired. I shivered in bed, shutting myself off from the world, trying to not think of anything, because everything was too much, attempting to will myself into a numbing slumber, but I couldn't.

Wouldn't.

Didn't.

That's when the voice, after months of silence, returned to me.

"Seek."

That's all it said. Nothing more, nothing less. First: *Look.* Then: *Go.* Now: *Seek.* But seek *what?* For that matter, look at *what?* And go *where?*

Sitting up, I looked around, scoping for the origins of the voice.

A next-door neighbor?

A radio somewhere?

A TV?

Nothing. Couldn't there have been something else? A tad more detail than a trio of monosyllabic inscrutable commands? A full sentence would have been helpful. A face with a name, even better. An instruction book, an encyclopedia, a compendium—anything.

For a split second, I recalled the tome of a book handed over by Vera's alleged brother—the bearded fisherman in the village—the man with the Bible. Shrugged it off.

A knock at the door.

That's better. Come on in. Reveal yourself. Make yourself at home before I'm evicted. This boded well. A conversation might be had. An elucidation of sorts.

Another door knock.

Fine. I waited. Nothing happened.

A third knock.

"*What?*" I finally threw out there, a trifle annoyed the voice didn't just let itself in.

"It's me" came a voice from the other side.

"You'll have to be a bit more specific," I called out, my voice cracking from not having been used in days.

"It's Tally," she said. "Remember me? Your *sister.*"

A discovery: The door knock was real. Disappointment prevailed.

Climbing out of bed, I trudged to the front door, sidestepping an obstacle course of empty moving boxes, and let Tally in.

"Thought you were someone else," I said, retreating to the bed and assuming a flattened position.

"Who?" she asked at the threshold, decked out in a power suit and holding a wad of envelopes.

(God?)

"Never mind," I said, shoving my face in a pillow. "Close the door on your way out."

Per usual, judging by her footsteps, Tally ignored my request, doing what she wanted, which was to venture further inside the muck of my apartment—and life.

"I stopped by because you haven't been answering your phone," she said.

Lifting my head, I asked, "Is there a question embedded in that statement?"

"I wanted to make sure you were—"

"—Not dead?"

"That you were okay."

"I'm just dandy," I said in a monotone.

"Plus, I brought in your mail," Tally said. "Still have your mailbox key. You never picked it up after your trip to Mexico."

*Mexico.*

Why'd she bring that up? My latest fiasco of a harebrained scheme born of pure idiocy.

"When," she asked, "was the last time you checked your mailbox?"

Let me see . . . "What year is this?" I replied, scratching my unwieldy beard.

Tally didn't dignify my question of her question with an answer, instead dumping a pile of unopened letters on the futon next to my prone body.

"You can stay at my place after you pack up your stuff," she said without looking at me, without mentioning the nasty word, the direct cause of the stuff that needed to be packed up: eviction.

I didn't look at her either. I looked at the clock. It read: 11:11.

Again.

Why was it always 11:11?

What did it mean?

Tally started busying herself by straightening out the apartment.

"Leave it alone," I croaked.

"Leave what alone?" She looked up.

"The mess," I said. (Translation: My life.)

While I sunk my face back into the pillow, Tally kept cleaning before she darted over, grabbed a thick manila envelope with an official-looking return address, and tossed it at my head.

"Open this one," she ordered. "It might be important."

I didn't move. I couldn't help hearing the sound effects, though: a big Tally sigh. Followed by the tearing open of the envelope.

"You better look at this," she said, nudging me with urgency.

I knew better than to ignore Tally when she was in such a state. A nudge could turn into a knock, which could morph into a hit upside my head. Some things don't change, even after the end of a shared childhood with an irrepressible sister. Reluctantly, I turned myself over and grabbed the stack of papers Tally had just unsheathed from the manila envelope. Muscle memory locked in. Professional habits overtook me. I recognized what it was right away: the response from the police in Skiatook to my Freedom of Information Act request for public records. The FOIA. Had completely forgotten about it. It almost felt like another life ago. It was, in a way. Months had fallen by the wayside since I had submitted that request. Before all the stops and starts. Before Mexico. Before Luke and all the rest. But here it was: the answer. In my hands rested a swath of photocopies of decade-old police records: incident reports, supplemental reports, a dense array of tortured English phraseology, typos, and observations gathered by police investigators about Maggie's case and the plight of her daughter, Mary.

As expected, much of what I scanned was boilerplate—a string of words copied and pasted here and there, signifying nothing.

But wait.

What was *that*?

My eye stopped at something a bit out of the norm. It was an old letter from the police detective leading the investigation into Maggie's case. The detective had written to some sort of colleague whose name had been redacted, blotted out in black, by the censors before they sent me this batch of old records.

The letter was dated November 11 a decade ago. That number again:

11/11/11

It wouldn't leave me alone. But that's not what halted me. What stopped me was what the detective wrote:

"Dear -------,

"There's a problem. I spoke with the main doctor who examined Mary at the hospital, and he isn't convinced she was the victim of abuse. Actually, it's the opposite. Dr. ------- thinks Mary has a vitamin D deficiency, causing rickets. Dr. ------- says that the condition explains the break of the bones found in the X-rays. Dr. ------- calls it 'brittle bones,' whatever that means. I know this is ridiculous, but Dr. ------- says what happened to Mary was likely the result of a 'short fall,' or something else 'benign.'

"Don't worry, though. I've found another medical expert, who I'm told will see things our way. I will let you know how it goes."

Suddenly, I could hear myself breathing unevenly. Two things.

First: This was what was commonly called "tunnel vision," when authorities are so sure they've nabbed the culprit, they fail to consider other possibilities, so focused are they on a conviction. Maybe no crime had occurred at all. More likely: It was an accident.

Second: This letter had never seen the light of day. That, I was sure of. I'd reviewed the trial transcript. There was never any mention of the primary doctor not only questioning whether Mary was the victim of abuse but positing that she was likely the victim of an accident, of a congenital condition involving brittle bones. That diagnosis was not presented at trial by the medical experts trotted out by the prosecution. *Au contraire:* They had insisted Mary was unquestionably the victim of physical abuse.

Actually, one other thing.

Third: When I submitted the FOIA request, someone evidently in the police records department didn't bother to actually read these decade-old documents. They must've simply mechanically printed out the records, redacted names, and dumped them in the mail.

Had they done otherwise, inspecting what the records showed, they might've thought better to prune one or two documents from view. But that's what happens when ten years pass by. People forget. Details get lost, including that the police had buried this letter all those years ago when it mattered. There was no other way of viewing it. Had the police detective's letter been provided to Maggie's court-appointed lawyer as part of the discovery process, which was the prosecution's legal obligation, her attorney would have surely presented it as part of her defense. I was no lawyer, but I knew enough from other investigations to understand what this meant: The prosecution had committed what is known as a Brady violation, withholding key evidence pointing to Maggie's innocence.

This was, to put it mildly, a violation of her right to due process. She'd been denied her constitutional right to a fair trial.

What wasn't definitive was whether anyone had committed a crime. But given what the unnamed doctor said in the redacted letter, it sure looked like it was merely an accident. I was flooded with what I'd heard in other wrongful convictions: that we want to believe the system works; that we want someone to pay for what we are convinced is a crime; that we accept a charge as fact when it might not be.

"What?"

I looked up, realizing Tally was still standing there in my constricting apartment, waiting to see what I had just discovered in the envelope.

"I don't think Maggie did it," I said.

"I thought you thought that already." Tally looked unsurprised.

"Well," I said, shaking the paper, "now it's looking more likely."

"Anything else?" Tally asked, arms folded.

"Looks like her daughter, Mary, had a preexisting medical condition that made her prone to bone fractures," I said.

"So, what happened to her was probably an accident?" Tally asked.

"That's what it appears."

"I guess Ram's off the hook, too," she said.

I hadn't thought of that: When I spoke to Maggie's ex-boyfriend in that courthouse parking lot weeks earlier, when he elbowed me in the face, he had practically confessed to a crime it looks like he didn't know he hadn't committed after all.

"Good point," I said, feeling an unexpected injection of adrenalin.

Tally gave me a self-satisfied smirk: "Told you so."

I didn't remember what Tally had told me about whether Ram was guilty or not, but I took her word for it. She was usually right.

"Well, does that settle it?" she asked, holding out a hand to help me get up from the futon.

Grabbing her hand, I managed to stand, light-headed: "Not quite."

# 36

The first order of business: I needed to figure out the redacted doctor's name. As it turned out, the task wasn't as challenging as I had anticipated. Finally, something easy to find.

While the doctor's name had been blacked out in the police documents, the physician's hospital address wasn't. It was right there at the top left side of the letter. All that was required was for me to do a little reverse engineering. I googled the hospital and clicked my way through a series of screens until I reached Suite 2-11, the doctor's office. Dr. Elijah's office, that is.

The next step was just as simple. I paid the good doctor a visit in Tulsa, just south of Skiatook.

Except he wasn't in. So informed the receptionist, who seemed perturbed that I had the audacity to show my face in the waiting room without an appointment.

The receptionist offered a terse "no" when I asked if the doctor could be expected back any time soon. Nothing else was forthcoming. The receptionist was Fort Knox wrapped tightly in the secrecy of the CIA. No way he was spilling any state secrets. Fine.

This was doable. Returning to the car rental, I fired up the laptop and tapped into a series of proprietary databases, to look up every Elijah in the book. Cross-referenced every positive hit with each Elijah who happened to be a doctor. Then narrowed the search to those inhabiting Oklahoma. Presto.

There he was. Maybe ten minutes away. It was quite simple. I drove over there. And confronted a prosperous home.

Just as I stepped up to the front door and prepared to knock, I girded myself for an unpleasant reception. Good thing I brought along a prop—a copy of the police records produced from my FOIA request—flapping in an envelope by my side. It might distract the doctor long enough to take note, wonder about its contents, and consider hearing me out. Not much of a strategy. But it's what I had.

A sliver of a face showed from the front door opened just a crack.

"Can I help you?"

I hadn't even knocked yet. He was already one step ahead of me.

It wasn't a friendly face. It wasn't *not* a friendly face. It was wizened and clinically inquisitive as if I were a specimen under a microscope.

"Dr. Elijah," I began.

"Yes?"

And here's when I upchucked the whole story—the abridged version—about how I'd come across his dubious diagnosis of Mary's symptoms. That it likely wasn't a case of abuse but of a vitamin D deficiency resulting in brittle bones that may have caused fractures as a result of a short fall or something else benign, and I was sure to use that word, *benign*, hoping it might jog his recollection.

"Ah," he said.

Side note: Dr. Elijah hadn't opened the door any further. Nor had he unlatched the sliding chain keeping me out. I was on unspoken probation.

"Well, I've examined thousands of cases," the doctor said circumspectly. "But, yes, I do happen to remember that particular case."

After describing who I was (that is, a friend of Maggie, *yadayadaya*), I let the brief silence between us marinate until the physician warmed himself up enough to resume where he'd left off.

"Not to be macabre about this, but had there been abuse involved, there would have been grip marks on the body," Dr. Elijah said dispassionately. "There would have been bruising indicating the child was roughly handled. There were, in fact, one or two bruises, but only of a minor variety, surface contusions, but nothing to indicate the kind of violent force, the torque, if you will, necessary to inflict significant damage."

"I see," I said. (The less I said, the better. He needed no encouragement.)

"What's more," Dr. Elijah said, raising an index finger, "given the characteristics of the subdural hematoma."

"The what?"

"The brain bleed," he said, giving off a slight air of irritation at my medical ignorance. "It would have required a tremendous amount of shaking action that would have likely injured or broken the neck."

"And there was no broken neck?" I posited, trying to keep up.

"Correct," the doctor said. "Not even close. The neck was perfectly intact."

"Then what caused the brain bleed?" I asked, worried I was overlooking the obvious.

Dr. Elijah held his gaze on me. "That's the first intelligent question you've asked, young man."

That was the first time I'd been called a young man in a while. "Thank you," I said, quite unsure if a thank you was in order for the age reference or my hiatus from obtuseness.

Dr. Elijah seemed to be loosening up, as if issuing a lecture: "A subdural hematoma—a brain bleed—offers a variety of differential diagnoses."

Back to dumb: "Meaning what?" I asked.

"There could be a number of causes," he said. "A short fall. A rare condition. A congenital matter. Trauma to the child's head as it passed through the birth canal. We know, for instance, the mother in this instance experienced a difficult delivery."

The mother—a nonpersonal pronoun—Maggie.

"Same with the retinal hemorrhaging," Dr. Elijah noted.

More stumbling: "You mean?"

"The bleeding within the eyes," he said with a beleaguered sigh.

"Right," I said as if I had known all along what he was talking about.

"There's debate in the medical community about the cause

of such eye damage," he said. "Some of my professional colleagues are of the opinion that retinal hemorrhaging of a specific nature must be the result of violent shaking. But others, and I include myself in this camp, have studied the issue and have concluded such eye damage could be the result of a number of other factors."

I was lost in the weeds. "What," I asked, "does it all mean?"

The doctor stared at me dourly. "It means, young man: Who knows for sure?"

"Who knows?" I echoed.

"Correct," he said. "Sometimes, medicine is more art than science. We don't have all the answers—far from it. Some of it is a matter of educated guesses. Sometimes, we're dead wrong. Remember when doctors used to recommend infants rest on their stomachs?"

I didn't know babies existed yet, except for Tally's. They didn't inhabit my sphere other than as an abstraction.

"No," I admitted. "I didn't know that."

"Well," he said, "doctors used to think it was safer for infants to sleep on their stomachs until they didn't. Eventually, doctors reversed themselves and said it was safer for infants to sleep on their backs."

"The complete opposite," I said for confirmation.

"Exactly."

"That doesn't give me a lot of confidence in the profession," I professed.

"Sometimes, we're groping in the dark," Dr. Elijah said. "That is certainly the case when we're dealing with an infant who couldn't speak for herself, where there were no witnesses to any alleged abuse, and the symptoms were far from definitive."

The upshot: The doctor wasn't saying Maggie was innocent. He wasn't saying she wasn't *not* innocent either. He was saying he didn't know for sure. It was a lot to take in. And not exactly what I wanted to hear, if I could be honest with myself for a moment (always a challenge).

"What do I do with this?" I asked the question aloud but it was more meant for myself.

Dr. Elijah shrugged. "All I can tell you is that I carefully examined that child and I wasn't convinced she was the victim of abuse or neglect; indeed, the evidence pointed in a different direction, given her medical history—the vitamin D deficiency, the rickets, the brittle bones, the mother's complicated delivery. There was no way I could diagnose the child as the victim of abuse. The likelihood, medically speaking, was that no one was to blame."

"Right," I said glumly.

Equivocation had that effect on me. It was uncomfortable to consider that Maggie wasn't entirely cleared of neglect or any other wrongdoing by what the doctor had just said. I didn't want to believe she had done anything wrong—still didn't think she had. But it wasn't definitive. Dr. Elijah couldn't provide that certainty—that absolution. Based on his best medical assessment, there was a benign cause to Mary's symptoms. I would just have to take it on faith.

"You need to remember something," he said, intruding on my thoughts.

"Yes?"

"Doctors are healers," he said. "We are not police. We don't solve crimes. That, in my estimation, should be left for others."

"Hm," I grunted.

"And," he added, "for whatever it's worth, nobody seemed to want to listen to what I had to say anyway. That, I'll never forget."

With that, the good doctor softly shut the door without so much as a goodbye. I continued to stand there, as if not quite catching up to the present, staring at the closed door. Because I wasn't in the now. I was still cogitating on that last bit from the doctor, his delicate implication that authorities had dismissed his diagnosis of Mary. That they hadn't listened to him. That he hadn't been convinced abuse or neglect were involved. Let me rephrase that more concretely, as per my journalistic training: That Mary hadn't been the victim of violence. The doctor pointed to a more likely alternative explanation—an explanation, by the way, that I'd never heard before, that had never been raised at trial, about brittle bones, that had never been known by the defense, by Maggie, because the police detective's letter had been buried until it had come to light only now—I was about to say miraculously—serendipitously.

However it came to be, there it was, the revelation, in my request for public records from the police department. The police detective's letter. Exposing doubt. Shielded from view, the letter demonstrated that the authorities knew there were grave doubts about whether Maggie had committed a crime—whether there was any crime at all—and yet, they had hidden that fact and sought out other experts who conformed to their suspicions. Simply put, Maggie had been deprived of a fundamental right—vital information that could have changed the course of her trial a decade earlier. This undeniable fact shed light on at least one thing: the fallibility of the legal system, and the messiness of the idea of justice.

But did she do it? She was, after all, not convicted of abuse. No one was. She was punished for what the jury determined was a matter of criminal neglect. It was, I suppose, unknowable—barring a confession, and even then, studies show that the accused, under duress, sometimes confessed to crimes they didn't commit. That I had reservations caused discomfort; I felt bad for questioning, even remotely, Maggie's innocence. In the end, I would have to make a choice—and I chose to believe her. This single act was within my control.

But leaving that aside, I took hold of a more practical consideration: Did the newly discovered police letter in my trembling hands offer enough legal justification to set Maggie free?

# 37

Events tumbled forward with interconnected intent: I wrote to Maggie, telling her all that I had discovered, including the police letter she never knew about; Maggie in turn told her mama, who promptly pivoted and hired an attorney to do something about it; and I fell by the wayside, decamping to Tally's place, temporarily making myself at home on her living room couch. She had the decency not to question my lingering presence. Abby, her curious child, offered even less resistance. I was a newfangled toy.

It's amazing how little can occur over so much time while couch surfing. I woke up late, and fell asleep early, waiting for the day to end again. Maggie, for her part, had already lost at trial a decade earlier. The appellate court had already affirmed her conviction not much later. She was out of regular appeals. But now her lawyer filed a petition in federal court for a writ of habeas corpus, a challenge to her imprisonment based on the letter I had discovered. Her attorney, entering the letter into evidence, argued that the authorities had failed in their duty to furnish Maggie's defense with this crucial piece of evidence by not revealing the doctor who performed the autopsy on her child believed Mary suffered from a vitamin D deficiency; the doctor wasn't convinced it was a case of abuse or neglect. Maggie's attorney called the omission of the police detective's letter a clear Brady violation—a withholding of exculpatory evidence at trial. She should be set free, he asserted.

In response, prosecutors dismissed the letter as much ado about little but an opinion of one doctor. She should remain locked up, they countered.

Such was the situation, according to a steady stream of calls from Maggie's mama, who kept me informed about the legal jousting back and forth, motions of inexplicable verbiage filling electronic files.

Meanwhile, I plunged deeper into a dark cesspool of drink and drugs. Tally gave me death stares. She flushed my prescription pills down the toilet. She threw out my bottles of whiskey. I merely obtained more of both on overdrawn credit and reclined on the couch until merrily passing out. It was a job, of sorts. Okay, maybe an avocation.

Abby, Tally's infant daughter, built little forts around my prone body. I served as the foundation for a display of dinosaurs enjoying a picnic. She crawled over my back to reach for a toy set of plastic sushi: salmon, fish eggs, and eel. Tally arrived home late from work and, per custom and politeness, asked how my day was, as if I had actually done something of utilitarian value. I grunted nonspecifically and explored no alternatives. Why bother? This—the couch, the array of infant toys about my person—sufficed as a life until it was mercifully over. My general perspective was that of the close-up view of fibers of the blanket I usually draped over my benumbed face, to shield myself from daylight and the busybodies of the known querulous world. Thoughts flicked from Pablo to Vera to Enos to Luke, but I returned to Maggie, always.

She had a chance, maybe, finally—a path forward beyond prison—if the court took action. And then it came to pass. Tally was the one who brought this to my attention, poking me awake on the couch and shoving a crisp copy of the *Herald* in my bewildered face. The headline on page 27 of the tabloid, my former employer, blared:

### JUDGE EXCORIATES PROSECUTION; MOM'S CONVICTION MAY BE OVERTURNED

The federal judge overseeing the proceedings—presidentially appointed to a life sentence on the bench and thus immune to the vicissitudes of politics and the impolitic—had weighed in on Maggie's case. Issuing a 77-page opinion, the judge called her conviction "a manifest injustice."

The judge said a lot of other things, calling into question the entire diagnosis of cases like hers involving caregivers—mothers, mostly—who were accused of what was known as shaken baby syndrome. The judge excoriated those who didn't consider emerging science and medicine that offered alternative explanations for the triad of symptoms typically associated with the syndrome: brain bleeding, brain swelling, and bleeding within the eyes. And he took the prosecutors to task for failing to hand over to the defense at trial the police detective's letter showing the doctor didn't believe abuse had occurred. The judge threw out big weighty terms like "fundamental rights" and "due process" and the affirmation of a "Brady violation."

It all amounted to one thing: It looked like Maggie might actually be set free. I sat there, not quite comprehending what I was reading in the newspaper. For a split second, I was confused about what was real and what wasn't. It was like having a delayed reaction to the rumblings beneath you while the earth shakes and only a few seconds later do you realize you're smack dab in the middle of an earthquake, the real thing. After everything, after the excursions to Skiatook, the cemetery, the courthouse, the visits to Enos, the forays into Mexico, the doubts, the failures, the lost leads, and everything else that this pursuit entailed, it had finally come to this denouement. Maybe I was in a state of shock; my emotions were still trying to catch up to the facts printed before me in the *Herald*. I took another look at the article. My name wasn't mentioned but there was a reference that someone had discovered the decade-old police detective's letter through a Freedom of Information Act request for public records, which had broken open Maggie's case.

"Justice must be served," her attorney was quoted as crowing, urging the judge to take the last consequential step and set his client free.

*Justice.* What did that word mean, anyway? Even if Maggie wasn't innocent, she had already served a decade in prison for neglect. Wasn't that enough? Hadn't she paid the price, and dearly?

Too complicated for my shriveled brain, suffused under the influence of intoxicating drinks and mind-altering substances. I chose to believe Maggie was innocent. Who was I to judge anyway? Are we—any of us—defined solely by the worst act we've ever committed?

Maggie, by the way, was voiceless in the news article. "The prisoner could not be reached for comment," the *Herald* noted. As I sat back on the couch, the words on the page blurred into a dissolve. This, I had to admit, was epic, the prospect of Maggie walking free. And if I'm being fully candid, there was a small part of me that couldn't help wondering whether this is what an authentic miracle looked like on paper, in black-and-white.

# 38

Dear Joe,

Thank you. Thank you so much. I wish I could say it better, tell it to you in a way that you'd know how much my heart is bursting.

Still hard to believe, but I might actually get out of here. I'm already imagining what I might do on the outside first. One real possibility: There's this place called "The Feast" not too far from my mama's place in Skiatook. Buffet-style. All you can eat.

After that, who knows?

In your letters, you've never told me about where you stand when it comes to faith. If you don't mind my saying, I sense there's a struggle. But please know this, Joe. I always believed there was a way, a future, and a hope beyond these walls. God placed you in my life. You were the instrument of my deliverance. This is just the beginning. He has big plans for you.

One other thing: I've always looked forward to your letters and what's inside them, especially your wild adventures to who knows where. Your letters, they're like little gifts, care packages, from beyond. My letters to you are meant in the same way, a present of myself to you.

But there's something I'd been meaning to mention for some time. Not sure why I've held back. But there's no reason anymore. You don't have to write to me anymore. Not just because it looks like I may be getting out soon. It's because letters aren't necessary. Maybe you didn't know this, but instead of writing, I can call you on the telephone in my pod if you write your number in your next letter to me. I have a few bucks on my account. The telephone's located in the dayroom. There's not a lot of privacy. You'll hear a racket in the background. But I'd get a chance to hear your voice. And you'd hear mine. I'd like that.

Blessings,

Maggie

# 39

Maggie found me, even though I wasn't where she thought I was.

Or rather, her letter found me, though having been evicted, I wasn't inhabiting my box of an apartment anymore. The postal system forwarded my mail to Tally's place—no doubt with my sister's scurrilous aid in filling out a change-of-address form. Whether the sender of the letter was also notified of my change of address, I didn't know. But, for what it was worth, I did know how this all generally worked. I'd helped other inmates gain their freedom; I'd chatted with them a lot. I was aware how the prison telephone system worked before Maggie mentioned it. But I'd never brought it up with her for one simple reason: I preferred to think of her as the last person in the wired world without access to a bloody phone.

I'd gotten used to the Victorian habit of conversing by the written word with Maggie. Things were so curated and repressed. Emotions were always subtext. There was comfort in the *not* knowing, the *not* expressing, in the subtlety of thinking before articulating. What was left was an attempt to detect personality in the curvature of the handwriting, the looping of a J, the swooping of a Y. Sometimes, my hand would cramp from the effort. It wasn't used to the exertion; fingers had been accustomed to tapping on a keyboard, nearly in silence. In my letters, Maggie couldn't hear the plaintive yearnings in my tremulous voice. I couldn't say the wrong thing without knowing it. I wouldn't overshoot with the wrong comment placed too early in a conversation. It was better that she couldn't see me for who I was. It was cleaner. Neater. Safer in a nineteenth-century kind of way. In my letters, I could still maintain a modicum of normalcy. I could be the person I wanted to be, the person she envisaged.

All of which is another way of saying I didn't send her my phone number. For the first time, I didn't write back to Maggie. Some things, I decided, were better left unsaid. It was time to let go.

# 40

"Enos is dead."

That's how Maggie's mama started the call when she phoned me. No, "How are you?" No, "What's going on with you?" She was never one for the usual pleasantries. She was always in an egg-timer rush. Maybe she had an apple pie baking in the oven. Even so, it was startling to hear her utter the stark words without prologue.

For a moment, I couldn't quite place Enos, but his drawl came back, followed by his connection: the old friend of Luke, who had helped fake the car crash decades ago. The one who led me to Mexico.

"What happened?" I asked.

"Car crusher," she said.

"Sorry?"

"His body was found flattened like a pancake in the compactor at the junkyard next to his shack," she said unemotively.

"*What?*"

"Yep," she said. "The hydraulic machine. Somehow or other, they think Enos got drunk and stumbled into the compactor that crushes derelict cars."

*Derelict.* Good word. The writer in me added a fictitious point in the air for Maggie's mama. She was always full of surprises. Then I was struck with a bout of guilt; how could I revert to the felicity of a word at a time like this? What was wrong with me, intellectualizing the minutiae in the face of tragedy?

"I'm sorry" was all I could say, not quite digesting what she had just said.

"There was alcohol in his system," she said. "There was always liquor in that man, like fuel in a vehicle. But they think it was an *accident.*"

I could hear the sneer in her voice.

"You don't think it was an accident?" I asked.

There was a pause on the other end of the line before she resumed.

"Enos had been operating that big ol' machine for years," she said.

"Meaning?"

"Meaning he could push the right button in his sleep, no problem."

Now it was my turn to say nothing. The import of what she was suggesting was already sinking in. Maybe this was my fault. Maybe if I hadn't pushed so hard, if I hadn't persuaded Enos to tell me the truth, if he hadn't revealed what had really happened with Luke and the staged car wreck, Enos would still be around.

If, if, if.

"Think about it," Maggie's mama said. "He woulda had to push the button, run around the contraption and slip himself in the bed of the machine before it crushed him to a pulp. Sound like something you'd do when you're drunk?"

(Possibly.)

"No," I said anyway.

"Sound like an accident to you?" she asked.

"No," I said again.

Playing back in my head the last conversation with Enos, I could hear him express no concerns whatsoever about the secret he was revealing to me. He was almost cavalier about it. He seemed more concerned about my welfare, not his own. There had been a veiled threat—maybe not so veiled—that if I didn't keep my mouth shut, harm could come to me. Not to him. Enos, however, did mention the cartel. He did mention the prospect of torture and death. The car crusher sounded like it held the promise of both.

Next, I retrieved what Luke had said—that he figured Enos was still working for the cartel as a drug runner, paying off the debt from what Luke had stolen. Maybe the debt had finally come due.

Or maybe this was an overactive thyroid. I mean, come on. Really? What, the cartel was actually monitoring Enos and overheard his conversation with me? And then crushed him to death?

Comforting myself, I preferred to think it was an accident. There was, as Maggie's mama pointed out, alcohol in his system. When there was a sufficient amount of drink in me, I was liable to do just about anything under the rubric of stupid, bordering on plain ridiculous.

"I told you so," Maggie's mama said with an edge in her voice.

"Told me what?"

"I told you," she scolded me, "about fixing to get involved in other people's business."

Not once on the telephone call did she breathe a word about her daughter, Maggie. She neglected that part. There was that word again.

*Neglect.*

# 41

Even in misery, there is routine. Mine began when I awoke on the living room couch and joined Abby in the construction of a fort comprised of pillows, blankets, and any other makeshift delights of an infant who was frankly way too cute for her own good.

Eventually, Abby grew tired of that mindless fort-building activity, which freed me to construct a cup of coffee and fetch the newspaper slipped under the front door. Yes, Abby's mother, my sister Tally, was among the last of the Mohicans with a subscription to a non-digital version of the *Herald*.

This, of course, annoyed me to no end because the presence of the hard copy of the newspaper only reminded me of my own ruination on a daily basis. Perhaps, though, I was a glutton for punishment. I couldn't quite resist leafing through the pages of my former employer—a habit of my prior life—while I sipped on a cup of coffee, perusing the blaring front page, gossip on page six, sports on the back. But, on this particular morning, just a day after the unexpected call from Maggie's mama about the abrupt death of Enos, I casually turned to a page with a singular anomaly.

A news brief:

## AMERICAN FAMILY SLAIN IN MEXICO

Details were sketchy but this much was reported: A husband and wife and their two adult sons, all ex-pats, were killed just outside of San Miguel. Execution-style. Authorities were investigating, but no suspects had been identified yet. No motive was known.

Steadying myself, I placed the steaming cup of coffee down on a side table. The cartel? Was that Luke and his family referenced in the article? Had Enos confessed, before being crushed to death, what he knew of Luke's whereabouts? It was possible the cartel tracked Luke down in Mexico and recovered the money he had stolen, or whatever was left of it. It was possible they exacted payment in the form of a bullet to the head, his and his family's. And yet this was more than I could fathom—too much for my conscience. It felt like an abstraction without the lurid entrails of the concrete. A coincidence?

Maybe I was reading too much into it. I didn't want to think about it. I cordoned off the thought. Shut the cabinet on the idea. I dropped the newspaper, splayed open, on the coffee table.

Maybe not.

In the margin of the newspaper, next to the news brief, as my mind reeled, I was drawn to a note scribbled with a pen in thick handwriting:

YOU'RE NEXT.

# 42

From the scrawled note, I could extrapolate certain facts: that Enos's death likely wasn't an accident. That the cartel had probably killed him. Not a giant deductive leap. He'd told me secrets. He had helped Luke fake his death after the absconding of cartel drug money; not a great recipe to avoid severe bodily harm. Furthermore, the execution-style killings outside San Miguel must've referenced Luke and his family. I was, after all, next.

This wasn't the first note. An echo from the recently departed past: *Don't come back.* Evidently, I didn't get the first hint.

Another extrapolation: They knew where I lived. What's more, they were coming after me. But why? Almost as soon as I asked myself the question, I answered it. I knew enough to be a nuisance. Tie up loose ends. Which meant what? Unknown to me, until now, the cartel must have been tracking my movements for some time.

A creak in the hardwood floors caused me to flinch. I could feel the tensile stress in my neck before I realized it was nothing, just the groans of pipes in an old apartment building on the Upper West Side. Not long after I had awoken, Tally had taken Abby for a Sunday stroll in Riverside Park. No one was home, except me. What, by the way, do I tell Tally? My sister might not take it well, how I'd brought great danger to her doorstep. I was still trying to figure out what to tell Tally about what had happened to Enos. The car crusher had just happened. Now, this. Luke and his whole family. Things were falling apart—or falling into place with dispatch—depending on the point of view. I would have to sort this out and decide on the precise words to impart to Tally. I'd have to leave. Where, though, could I go?

But first, an idle question arose: Why had the cartel warned me? Why not just sneak up behind me and lodge a bullet in the back of my head? So much easier. Quicker. What was the point of flushing me out?

An awareness: I wasn't afraid for myself. It was more like a mental exercise, a working out of things. I was so unafraid that I was concerned I wasn't afraid. It had come to this: a realization that death was coming to me—or for me. I didn't need to initiate the process. It wasn't on me anymore. No more dilly dallying.

A rapping of the front door interrupted my musings. In my T-shirt and shorts, I stepped over to the door and craned a look-see through the peephole. A familiar face. My shoulders relaxed.

What was *he* doing here?

I swung the door open, and there it was: the old Redskins ballcap. Ram was camped underneath it. Maggie's ex-boyfriend was as emaciated as ever.

"You gonna invite me in?" he asked, pulling up his droopy pants.

Twitching reflexively, Ram didn't wait for an answer, ambling into the apartment foyer, as if by right, like he owned the joint.

"What are you doing here?" I asked, shutting the door and joining him in the adjoining living room where he bivouacked. Ram slumped on the couch, ignoring my question. "Nice pad," he said, surveying the cushy surroundings.

"Not mine," I said, plopping down on an easy chair opposite him.

"Too bad," he said.

He eyed a small statue on a side table of a maternal figure embracing a child. No doubt, the figurine was superfluous; it served no utilitarian purpose in Ram's world. Maybe not in mine either.

It occurred to me that I happened to be sitting in Tally's favorite chair. I never sat in the easy chair. Shouldn't be sitting in it. But she was at the park with Abby, and the couch, my province, was occupied by an uninvited guest making himself at home, Ram.

"How'd you find me?" I asked.

Ram ignored that question, too.

"Like the note?" he asked.

"What note?"

Ram flicked his capped head in the direction of the

newspaper that I had left spread open on the coffee table between us.

"The note I wrote," he said. "Next to the article about the dead family in Mexico."

That article. That note. That dead family. *You're next.*

"That was *you?*" I stammered.

"Thought you'd appreciate the gesture," he grinned.

Not understanding, I stared at Ram, voiceless.

"Didn't you work for that newspaper?" he asked.

"Thanks for reminding me," I said, instantly wondering: *How'd he know that?* I hadn't brought up my former employer when he'd decked me with an elbow shot in the head in the courthouse parking lot.

"Thought you'd get a kick out of the message," he said, fishing for something in his jacket pocket. "The newspaper killed your career. Now, the newspaper is warning you about a real killing."

Ram, the poet. He knew even more: of my professional collapse.

Couldn't be good.

With that, he pulled out a six-inch, serrated hunting knife.

There was no threat in the way he held it. He wielded it just as carelessly as pulling out a cigarette to smoke. Hazardous—but only in the way it was applied. Why, though, did the knife have to be serrated? Wouldn't the plunging of six inches of tempered steel into my midsection do enough damage? We sat there, saying nothing, sizing each other up. I felt strangely numb. I remembered he was a former MMA fighter. But he appeared rather malnourished, more so than before. I imagined a flurry of kicks and karate chops. My only fear had nothing to do with me. I wondered how much time I had before Tally and Abby returned from the park.

"You should say something," Ram finally said. He was perspiring.

"You work for the cartel," I said as a statement even though it was a question.

"The pay ain't bad, and they're a major employer in Skiatook," Ram said, clearing his throat. "They want to know what you know."

I asked myself: What do I know? That Luke faked his own death. That Enos had helped Luke. Apparently, it had to do with stolen cartel cash. Not verified, however. Couldn't run with that. Not on the front page of the newspaper. Which was another way of saying, I didn't know much. Nothing really. Didn't even know myself.

"I know everything," I announced. It was like rounding to the nearest whole number. Ram wouldn't have believed anything else.

"That's what they figured," he said. He was fidgeting. "You know what this means, right?"

"Let's get on with it," I said, slumping in the unauthorized easy chair.

Ram stood, looking like he could teeter over if I poked him.

"This," he said, holding the hunting knife as if it were a dead weight, "is gonna hurt."

What was he acting at? A dentist? Giving me fair warning before stabbing me with a sharp instrument that was for my own good?

"Don't you have a gun?" I asked, sitting up straighter in the easy chair.

"Makes too much noise," he said. "Dude, we are in the middle of friggin' New York."

Now I was a dude. Hadn't I thought of him as a dude?

"Ever heard of a silencer?" I asked.

"Ever heard of expenses?" he retorted.

"I thought your bosses paid you well," I said.

Ram rolled his eyes at that, exasperated. For a moment, the exchange between us felt like two guys casually comparing grilling techniques—gas or charcoal.

"Okay, fine," I said.

My best chance was to get Ram to end me quickly and depart the premises before Tally and Abby returned from their walk in the park. To make sure they didn't bump into Ram. Yes, Tally would be mighty perturbed, at a minimum, about the bloody mess, but some things couldn't be avoided. She could purchase a new easy chair for herself.

Here's the bright side: Abby wouldn't remember a thing. One of the benefits of being an infant. Short-term memory. It's all a haze.

"Sorry about this," Ram said, approaching me. "Just doing my job."

I hated when people said that. It was only slightly less annoying when people said it wasn't personal. Everything was personal.

"Thanks," I said, though, and I meant it.

Ram hesitated. "Thanks for what?"

How do I explain this? There was too much context to get him up to speed about the decline and fall of me. As I opened my mouth, but before the words formed, the front door swung open, and there they were: Tally, clutching a stroller containing Abby.

Tally caught sight of the glint of the knife first, then her gaze pivoted to Ram before it rested on me sitting in her easy chair.

"Forgot diapers," she said haltingly.

In rapid succession, words overlapping:

Me: "Get out of here."

Ram: "Don't go anywhere."

Tally: "We're not going anywhere."

*We.* I suppose Tally was including Abby in her plural defiance, although the child was hidden under the lid of the stroller, evidently sound asleep.

"You didn't quite plan this out?" I scoffed in Ram's direction.

Death had been taking its time. But now that I was confronting the concept of the end up close, away from my former box of an apartment, departed from my journey to Mexico, I couldn't help feeling the tentacles of discomfiture. Was it that I didn't want to die after all? Had I been fooling myself all along? Or was I just scared? Not ready? Or was I only worried about Tally and Abby since they had so rudely interrupted my imminent demise?

The real problem: I couldn't see how Ram could take care of me without doing the same with Tally. Maybe even Abby. Tally had seen his face. Ram could be identified. He had no alternative. He was boxed in. Which left me with no alternative either. I needed to do something. I couldn't let this happen. Not to Tally. Not to Abby.

"You didn't hurt Mary," I blurted out.

"*What?*" Ram recoiled.

It seemed like a non sequitur, bringing up Ram's child—Mary—at this delicate moment that had nothing to do with her. And yet. There it was. Who knew how the mind worked?

"It was an accident," I said.

Standing in the foyer, her hands gripping the stroller, Tally nodded her head knowingly at me. In sibling confidence, I could see she was already leaping two steps ahead of me, as usual.

"What're you talking about?" Ram was disoriented.

"What happened to your child, it was no one's fault," Tally said, shifting to her corporate voice, interceding before I could think to explain more because Tally already knew the story.

Something within Ram rewound as if trying to remember a locked memory.

"How do you know?" Ram asked, turning to Tally.

"Don't you read the papers?" she said.

"It was all over the news," I stepped in, rising from the easy chair. "A police detective's letter was recently discovered. It showed that the doctor who conducted the autopsy of Mary determined her injuries were the result of a vitamin D deficiency—not abuse. Brittle bones."

I conveniently left out one word: *likely*. As in: The child's injuries were *likely* the result of a preexisting medical condition—not definitively. Small detail. This, though, was not quite the milieu to describe nuance, not with a hunting knife in the offing.

Ram looked dubious. I sensed he wanted to believe, the way he continued to twitch. But he'd held onto this haunting for so long, it wasn't letting go of him quite yet. All this time, Ram had harbored the dread that he had roughly handled his child and let Maggie take the blame.

"This better not be some game you're playing at," Ram said, waving the hunting knife at me and Tally.

"It's no game," Tally said. She was still clutching the stroller.

"Do you still have that article?" I asked her.

"As a matter of fact, I do," Tally said. "It's in the album."

Album? Tally released the stroller and took a few steps, reaching out for a photo album resting on top of the upright piano by the front door.

"Your greatest hits," she said to me, retrieving the leatherbound book. "Over the years, I've been keeping an album of your investigations."

The album looked ready to burst, too thick to account for my investigations. Yellowed news clippings spewed out from the edges. I didn't know about the album. She'd never said anything about it.

I didn't know what to say.

Tally shrugged. Quite a time to mention this. We'd have to discuss this later—if there was a later. Meanwhile, Tally crossed from the foyer into the living room, stepped forward, a corporate barracuda displaying no fear of the hunting knife hanging loose from Ram's right hand, and showed him the album. She proceeded to flip open the album to one of the last pages, showing a taped newspaper clipping under a flimsy plastic covering.

"There," she said. "Take a look at that."

Ram complied, his eyes hungrily devouring the page before him.

Finally, he looked up, stunned.

"I always thought—" he started and stopped, a quiver in his voice. "Part of me wondered whether—" He stopped himself again, his eyes watering.

Time has a way of playing tricks on the mind. He was stoned and drunk back then, and let's face it, he had a knack for violence.

Neither Tally nor I said a word. Ram readjusted his Redskins cap. He pulled up his droopy pants. He cleared his throat. "Well," he said, "Whaddaya know?"

# 43

I wasn't dead yet.

It was only a matter of time, an inevitability. But that I was still alive might've been a technicality. I remained on the cartel's hit list. There was still a bounty on my head. They wanted me ended. They just didn't know where I was anymore. That's because, in a matter of hours after Ram's unexpected appearance with the hunting knife, I'd hastily left Tally's apartment.

Before long, I was tooling around in a used RV, parking the old monstrosity in various and sundry parks in random places further and further away from New York, the skyline of soaring skyscrapers growing distant until they disappeared, replaced by open sky.

The mobile home boasted a small kitchenette, which was

just fine for a microwaving fool like me. Sometimes, if I planned well enough, scouting out locations as the days and nights lapped by, I even found a temporary parking spot with a partial water view.

This form of living transportation was Tally's brainstorm. She figured I'd stay undead as long as I kept moving, driving from one anonymous place to another. I owed her sixty payments on this clunker of an RV. She didn't drive a hard bargain. She fronted me the first payment. The rest was a no-interest loan, to be paid "whenever." Her words.

I took to the wobbly caravan with surprising alacrity. I liked not being in one place. I didn't need much space. The outdoors was quite enough. I embraced the anonymity, the unceasing new stimuli, the mist of a predawn skyline, the solitude.

In the days that followed, no one came to pay Tally a visit. Which was just as well, given the 9mm semiautomatic she kept locked and loaded. Once, she thought she may have spotted a lookout on the corner, down the block from her apartment, but she couldn't be sure. There were plenty of suspicious characters hanging around doing nothing in the neighborhood. This was, after all, New York City.

Then again, the thinking was, the cartel wouldn't want to draw undue attention by going after a pretty prominent family member in the upper middle of Manhattan. Tally worked at a high pay grade. The cartel would simply try to hunt me down, according to conventional wisdom. Which is why I'd discarded my smartphone. I'd buy burner phones at the occasional Walmart I'd come across on the road. Use it, dump it. One thing, though, I couldn't get rid of: Ram.

Yes, he was firmly lodged with me in the RV. He had

insisted. Pleaded is more like it. After he didn't kill me, he made the quite convincing case that he needed to go into hiding too—or else he'd be killed himself. He hadn't fulfilled his contract killing. The cartel would be none too pleased by his lack of follow-through. He needed safe harbor. Ram had eagerly handed me the serrated six-inch hunting blade, placing it in my hand, handle first.

"Take me with you," he had implored.

Tally had given me a look as if to say: Are you *crazy*?

I had given her a look as if to retort: Yes, a bit.

Besides, Ram had made the further point that he had no viable income, and no career prospects, now that he had failed as a cartel killer.

He didn't have what he called "a real job."

Hard to argue with that. Not to mention, we couldn't leave him to die. Could we? Tally might, judging from her indeterminate frown.

But when I had thought about it, I had to admit, I'd taken a shine to Ram from the moment we met when he shoved an elbow in my face back in the courthouse parking lot. He wasn't a bad guy. Misguided, maybe. A thug, even. But not all bad. Who is?

Ram was just lost. Kind of like me. I think I understood his suffering. I believe I knew his anguish, in the pit. It might've been a stretch, but we were kindred spirits, unfixable, tumbling backward through the rabbit hole.

Ram also had made the somewhat reasonable case that he'd sleep on the RV's couch, reserving the not-so-plush bed for me. I wouldn't even know he was there. He had professed he didn't snore. That's what he had insisted.

"I guarantee it," he had stressed.

Out of earshot, Tally had tried to warn me that Ram might kill me in my sleep. I shrugged. "Why would he do that?" Another thought I didn't share with Tally: *So what if he did?*

"Maybe," Tally had surmised, "he's still working for the cartel."

"Really?"

"Okay, maybe not," she had said, once she pondered it properly. There was something about Ram that spoke of his recalcitrance; his endemic inability to do something permanent, to carry out what the cartel had requested of him. He was, as he confided later, merely a drug courier, not a contract killer, even if he possessed a proclivity for disproportionate violence. Still later, reinforcing his argument, I learned he collected rocks in the shape of elephants. Can you imagine how rare those are? And what did that tell me about Ram's true nature?

There was this, too: I couldn't in good conscience get rid of him. He had nowhere to go. This is what happens when you're not killed by the person who's supposed to kill you. I guess this is how friendships are formed. You begin by bunking in a rickety RV with a murderous sociopath if he decides not to fillet you to death.

Besides, I didn't have to make any permanent decisions. He could stay awhile.

# 44

I had no idea how we'd get by. We didn't have much liquidity between us. Actually, Ram had more money than I did, a sweaty wad of cash that amounted to $1,111. I didn't want to know where he got that stash. It was mostly in twenty-dollar bills. And there was that number again: 1,111, split by a comma instead of a colon but the same digits nonetheless: 1111. Whatever that meant.

This much I knew: The money wouldn't last long, not with the cost of gas and highway tolls and fast food; what's more, we couldn't use credit cards, not if we wanted to remain off the grid, undetectable from the cartel. Offhand, Ram suggested we mug senior citizens. He called it "easy pocket money." I thought he was kidding until I realized he wasn't. With a withering glare, I nipped that in the bud.

"Just tryin' to contribute," he said, backtracking into the rear of the RV.

This, I suppose, was the beginning of us getting to know each other. Not sure it would be terribly fruitful. We'd have to come up with some other way to make a living, something not just less morally questionable than forcibly removing money from the elderly but also less overt—that wouldn't call attention to ourselves. We needed to stay invisible. Ram got that. I'll give him this, though. He was a pretty neat roommate; he didn't let the dishes stack up. Had to appreciate that. It also turned out he was something of a reader. I didn't quite approve of his choice of literature, which was comprised of a set of paperbacks he bought at a used bookstore where we made a pitstop just outside Pittsburgh. The racy covers spouted breathless titles about scandal and intrigue. Sometimes, Ram winced without provocation. It was a tick. I never referenced it aloud. Had a feeling it was a residue of his drug-infested past. We all had our crucibles.

So be it.

For my part, I didn't hear voices anymore—the voice, to be precise. It had been some time since I'd heard the last of the incantations: *Seek*. I never did figure out what it all meant. A trilogy of commands: *Look. Go. Seek*. That was it. Nothing more. I was left to listen to my own interior voice for now.

At one point, while navigating the RV, that voice of mine wondered whether there should be a visit to my father—on death row. San Quentin State Prison was a long way off, on the other coast. There was all manner of bureaucratic paperwork standing in the way. I'd have to send my father a letter, which I hadn't done in about forever. He'd have to send a visitor form back to me, which was complicated since I didn't have a postal address, given the mobile nature of my living arrangements. I'd have to fill out the form and send it to some yackety-yak prison administrator who'd do a background check on me. The whole ordeal gave me agita. Hence, the conclusion: Save the idea for another day.

I kept driving.

Ram was snoring in the back. Loudly. So much for his guarantee that he didn't snore, that I wouldn't notice he was there. Here. Anyway, we had other places to see. Big Sur, for one.

"You say something?" Ram asked, rousing himself from a nap on the RV couch behind me.

Had he heard my thoughts?

"How do you feel about visiting Big Sur?" I called over my shoulder while passing a slow-moving station wagon in the middle lane.

"Big *what*?" Ram had no idea what I was talking about.

"Never mind," I said. "It'll be a surprise for you when we get there."

It'd be a surprise for me as well. Never been to Big Sur. In my mind's eye, I pictured soaring cliffs, roaring ocean, and a quiet sunset, a place of peace where there was no past or present.

Ram sat up, groggy, redirecting the conversation. "Let me tell you about my people," he said, stretching, preparing for an impromptu speech.

"Your people?"

"The Cheyenne Nation," he declared, climbing up into the passenger seat. "Nomadic hunters."

I nodded, the writer in me appreciating the word: *Nomadic.* We were a bit nomadic ourselves, rumbling along on Interstate 70 West.

"Mighty warriors, my people," Ram continued, gazing out at the tapering highway before us. "Before the white man ruined everything."

Ram went on to recount the various conflicts and clashes between the Cheyenne Nation and the invading settlers from America and Europe. He gave me the full rundown of the failed Medicine Lodge Treaty of 1867. The disgrace of the Dawes Act of 1887. The travesty of the Land Run of 1892. And the dismantling of his great tribe with the Curtis Act of 1898. We'd nearly reached Topeka, Kansas, by the time Ram finished. He'd worn himself out.

"I guess I should feed the dog," he said.

Ah, right.

The dog.

About that: Let me back up. She happened to be a cross between a Mini Pinscher and a Chihuahua, a little thing with hues of black and brown in her coat and a tuft of white in her chest. Here's the thing. The other day, Ram and I had gotten lost somewhere around Terre Haute, Indiana, and found ourselves in the vicinity of a shelter, Orphan Dogs of the Storm. I knew we shouldn't have stopped in to take a look. Because that's all it took.

One look, and the next thing you knew, here we were with a permanent new addition, an adopted vicious little mutt named Rosie. Another roommate in the RV. There was hardly enough room for Ram and me. And now along came Rosie, who happened to spread out during naps, paws curled up, belly exposed. On my bed. She snored even louder than Ram did if that was possible.

Maggie had predicted I'd end up with a dog just like this.

Speaking of Maggie, the last time I heard from her was a couple of days ago when a letter from her arrived at my sister's place in New York. When I called Tally from a burner phone, I was just planning to say hi. She didn't say hi back. She went straight into the letter, reading aloud what Maggie had written to me.

With the phone in the crook of my neck, I asked Tally to speak slowly so I could take dictation, jotting down on a scrap of crumpled paper what I heard, to transcribe the words that Tally read, so that I could read back Maggie's letter when I needed to, to read between the lines, to soothe myself on the road.

# 45

Dear Joe,

I never heard back from you. It's okay. You're with me even when you're not.

I know it happened but I still can't quite grasp it: I'm free. Can't hardly remember the moment when I walked out of there.

All I remember about those first few moments was using a stainless-steel knife at "The Feast." Hadn't used a real knife in a decade. I ordered my first salad in ten years. I ate my first steak in over three thousand days.

The best part is, I've gotten to see Mary. Supervised visits, mind you. Martha, my cousin, hasn't told Mary who she is—that she's my daughter—not yet anyway. Not sure when that'll happen. All I can tell you is Mary is a beautiful little girl, all of eleven years old. She's still my daughter—but not. If you know what I mean. She lives with Martha in Skiatook, about ten minutes from my mama's place, where

I'm staying. When I've paid visits to Mary, I bring flowers picked off the side of the road. Dandelions are my favorites. We go for walks, Mary and me. She's been told I'm a distant relative, but I think she suspects something else. We kind of look alike. She even inherited my long toes, courtesy of my father. Truth is, we don't know each other. It's awkward, the silence between Mary and me. Life just goes along, as they used to say in the pod. I miss my friends there.

There's something else I need to tell you, Joe. I hope you don't mind. But it's on my heart. I have a friend at Mabel Bassett. She shouldn't be locked up. She was wrongfully convicted of murder. Life without parole. I just know she didn't do it. I've included her details on the attached sheet of paper, including her DOC number. She's easy to find. I've told her all about you. Well, not everything. But she's expecting to hear from you. Please help her, Joe. It's meant to be.

Blessings,

Maggie

P.S. I had another dream. We will meet again. I'm sure of it.

# 46

Dear Maggie,

I'm sorry I didn't call. I was going to say "never" but I don't like that word. Too extreme. Doesn't leave much room for a change of heart. I mean, who knows? Maybe one day.

Actually, I've been meaning to tell you something. I finally looked up "Skiatook." Always wondered what that meant—not just the town but the word itself. Do you know? It's Cherokee. Means "Big Indian Me." Or a big expanse of land. Or just plain big.

Somehow, it fits, wouldn't you say? It's all so big out there. Not just the place. It's so big, this life, it's impossible to see the outer limits. It's bigger than I can fathom—the good, the bad, the whole messy lot. It's beyond my comprehension what happened to you, what happened to me, what will happen, what it all means. All I can say is, maybe you're right. Maybe there is more to it than what we can see, what we can hear, what we can smell, what we can taste, what we can touch. How do we know there are only five senses? Maybe there's more.

As your mama may have mentioned, there have been some complications. It might involve some bad people who would like to see harm come to me. So, I've moved, and I keep moving. I don't have an address. I can't be found. Don't try to locate me. I'm a ghost.

But I know where you are. I know how to reach you. I will contact you again. That's a promise. But don't make anything of the return address of this letter of mine, whatever it might be. It's just a post office on the way to someplace else. You might, for instance, notice the postal address on the back of this envelope: Cawker City, Kansas. Yeah, I couldn't resist. It's pretty cool.

Please take good care of yourself, Maggie.

Yours truly,

Joe

P.S. You were right about the dog. Her name is Rosie. Vicious mutt.

# 47

What I didn't mention in my last letter to Maggie was the visit to the largest ball of twine in the world. Just happened to be in the neighborhood. Circumference: 40 feet, 3 inches; nearly 15,000 pounds. Took up a whole building next to a gas station in Cawker, Kansas. Surrounded by benches to ponder its enormity. One tourist tried to hug the ball. No way.

Not even close.

Ram was particularly taken with the epic ball of twine. With a disposable camera, he took a bunch of pictures. Not sure who he planned to share them with. Maybe no one.

I also failed to mention in my letter to Maggie anything about her friend in prison. The one she said was wrongfully convicted of murder, serving a life sentence without the possibility of parole. Otherwise known as LWOP. Maybe I didn't need to say anything about it. Maggie had a sense of things. For someone who had never laid eyes on me, she sure seemed to have me pegged. Because I was going to try to help her friend in trouble. It couldn't be helped. This is who I was. Who I am. Even mired in my own ruination, on the run.

Now, this also happened to apply to Ram as well. He didn't know it yet. But he was going to help me help this friend of Maggie's. Ram was coming along, whether he liked it or not. We were going to help this inmate, whoever she was. I was just waiting for the right moment to tell Ram, my compadre; maybe when we stopped at a rest stop to take in the setting sun and pray, a new habit of ours. I'm still not sure anyone is listening, but now at least I'm open to the possibility.

I also failed to mention to Maggie that her ex was now my roommate. Not sure that would have gone over terribly well. Didn't know how to broach the subject. But Ram was, in some way, my last and only connection to Maggie. He was, in a strange way, also a reminder of my own fragile mortality. It had been within his hands, literally, to put an end to me. I had wiggled my way out of that predicament, with Tally's steely guidance. I had argued against the dying light. There was still some fight left in me. Why? I contemplated that on the long stretches of asphalt whipping by, wondering if there was something else out there for me, some meaning, a refuge, a righteousness. I didn't imagine I'd find out until I did. I reserved the right to remain agnostic about the future. It would be what it will be, nothing more, nothing less. I just hoped I would rise to the occasion.

There was one last thing I didn't mention to Maggie in

my letter. But it was better this way—what was not said, how I felt. Real life was too chaotic, anyway; she was better off reconstructing her life on the outside without dealing with the shambles of me—a hunted man, who also happened to be destroyed. And if I was being fully candid with myself, there was this: that I wasn't worthy. It was more important that she not lose her good opinion of me than she learn of all my imperfections and foibles, a cataclysmic combination. That would be too much for me to bear. Maybe we'd meet some time. That's what I'd tell myself on the road. Maybe in another place. Maybe in another life, if there was such a thing. I was now open to the prospect.

Meanwhile, housed in the RV, I'd soothe myself with a recurring daydream: I'd reach out and hold Maggie's hand. Her palm would be sweaty in mine. She'd look at me shyly. I'd do the same. There would be anticipation but we'd let it linger. We'd step outside in the evening shadows under a crescent moon. Not sure where we'd be. Maybe in her mama's backyard. Didn't matter. Maggie would lead me to a quiet patch of soft grass, where we'd huddle close to each other in the darkness. I'd feel the sweet caress of her breath on my face, so close would she be to me. I'd want to tell her so much but I wouldn't be able to find the right words. Instead, I'd grasp a single wild daisy from the grass, pluck it, and hand it to Maggie, a silent gesture of my heart. She'd tuck the wild daisy above her right ear, shaded by her cascading hair. She wouldn't need to say anything. We'd sit there in silent harmony, letting go of the jagged past, understanding the promise of what was to come, looking up at the starry night in Skiatook, a vast canvas of infinity, where anything was possible, when anything could happen, where there was not just the Big Dipper but the faint contours of other images interlocked by the bright stars of the night sky, of hope, of a world beyond, of a grandness greater than anything imaginable.